CITY COME A-WALKIN'

ACITY COME A-WALKIN'

By **John Shirley**

Four Walls Eight Windows
New York/London

Published in the United States by:
Four Walls Eight Windows
39 West 14th Street, room 503
New York, N.Y., 10011

U.K. offices:
Four Walls Eight Windows/Turnaround
Unit 3, Olympia Trading Estate
Coburg Road, Wood Green
London N22 6TZ, England

Visit our website at http://www.4W8W.com

First printing December 2000

*This book has been revised from an earlier edition published in July, 1980 by
Dell Publishing. This edition was first released by Eyeball Books, 1996, which
kindly provided its design and typesetting to the present publisher.*

Book design and typography: S. Patrick Brown

Library of Congress Catalog Card Number: 96-84900

10 9 8 7 6 5 4 3 2 1

Printed in Canada

For every woman who ever had to put up with me

Foreword by

William Gibson

JOHN SHIRLEY WAS CYBERPUNK'S PATIENT ZERO, first locus of the virus, certifiably virulent. A Carrier. *City Come A-Walkin'* is evidence of that and more. (I was somewhat chagrined, rereading it recently, to see just how much of my own early work takes off from this one novel.)

Attention, academics: the city-avatars of *City* are probably the precursors both of sentient cyberspace and of the AIs in *Neuromancer,* and, yes, it certainly looks as though Molly's surgically-implanted silver shades were sampled from City's, the temples of his growing seamlessly into skin-stuff and skull. (Shirley himself soon became the proud owner of a pair of gold-framed Bausch & Lomb prescription aviators: Ur-mirrorshades.) The book's near-future, post-punk milieu seems cp to the max, neatly pre-dating *Bladerunner.*

So this is, quite literally, a seminal work; most of the elements of the unborn Movement swim here in opalescent swirls of Shirley's literary spunk.

That Oregon boy, with the silver glasses.

*　*　*

1

That Oregon boy remembered today with a lank forelock of dirty blond, around his neck a belt in some long-extinct mode of patent elastication, orange pigskin, fashionably rotted to reveal cruel links of rectilinear chrome spring: "Johnny Paranoid," convulsing like a galvanized frog on the plywood stage of some basement coffeehouse in Portland. Extraordinary, really. *And,* he said, he'd been to Clarion.

Was I impressed? You bet!

I met Shirley as I was starting to try to write fiction. Or rather, I had made a start, had abandoned the project of writing, and was shamed back into it by this person from Portland, point-man in a punk band, whose dayjob was writing science fiction. Finding Shirley when I did was absolutely pivotal to my career. He seemed totemic: there he was, lashing these fictions together and propping them in the Desert of the Norm, their hastily-formed but often wildly arresting limbs pointing the way to Other Places.

The very fact that a writer like Shirley could be published at all, however badly, was a sovereign antidote to the sinking feeling induced by skimming George Scithers' *Asimov's SF* at the corner drugstore. Published as a paperback original by Dell, in July 1980, *City Come A-Walkin'* came in well below the genre's radar. Set in a "near future" that felt oddly like the present (an effect I've been trying to master ever since), spiked with trademark Shirley obsessions (punk anti-culture, fascist vigilantes, panoptic surveillance systems, modes of ecstatic consciousness), *City* was less an sf novel set in a rock demimonde than a *rock gesture* that happened to be a paperback original.

Shirley made the plastic-covered Sears sofa that was the main body of Seventies sf recede wonderfully. Discovering his fiction was like hearing Patti Smith's *Horses* for the first time: the archetypal form passionately re-inhabited by a debauched yet strangely virginal practitioner, one whose very ability to do this *at all* was constantly thrown into question by the demands of what was in effect a shamanistic act. There is a similar ragged-ass derring-do, the sense of the artist burning to speak in tongues. They invoke their particular (and often overlapping, and indeed she *was* one of his) gods and plunge out of downscale teenage bedrooms, brandishing shards of imagery as peculiarly-shaped as prison shivs.

Mr. Shirley, who so carelessly shoved me toward the writing of stories, as into a frat-party swimming pool. Around him then a certain chaos, a sense of too many possibilities—and some of them, always, dangerous: that girlfriend, looking oddly like Tenniel's Alice, as she turned to scream the foulest undeserved abuse at the Puerto Rican stoop-drinkers, long after midnight in Alphabet City, the visitor from Vancouver frozen in utter and horrified disbelief.

"*Ignore* her, man," J.S. advised the Puerto Ricans, "she's all keyed up."

And, yes, she *was*. They tended to be, those Shirley girls.

I look at Shirley today, the grown man, who survived himself, and know doing that was *no mean feat*. A cat with extra lives.

What puzzles me now is how easily I took work like *City Come A-Walkin'* for granted. There was nothing else remotely like it, but that, I must have assumed, was because it was *John's* book, and there was no one remotely like John. Fizzing and crackling, its aura an ungodly electric aubergine, somewhere between neon and a day-old bruise, *City* was evidence of certain possibilities which had not yet, then, been named.

*   *   *

It would be a couple of years before whatever it was that was subsequently called cyberpunk began to percolate from places like Austin and Vancouver. Shirley was by then in whichever stage of a sequence of relationships (well, marriages actually; our boy was nothing if not a plunger) that would take him from New York to Paris, from Paris to Los Angeles (where he lives today), and on to San Francisco (hello, City). He gave me vertigo. I think we came to expect that of him, our tribal Strange Attractor, and blinked in amazement as he gradually brought his life in for a landing. Today he lives in the Valley, writing for film and television, but for several years now he has been rumored to be at work on a new book. I look forward to that. In the meantime, we have Eyeball Books to thank for re-issuing the Protoplasmic Mother of all cyberpunk novels, *City Come A-Walkin'*.

Vancouver, B.C.
March 31, 1996

City Come A-Walkin'

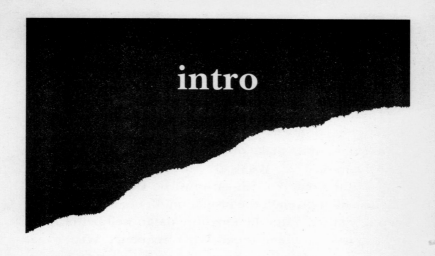

intro

A YOUNG WOMAN IN A recording studio adjusted her earphones and gave the engineer the signal. The engineer, on the other side of the booth's glass, nodded and pressed the button that would play the session back. She preferred the earphones.

The first song, hard improvisational rock—a style sometimes whimsically called *angst rock*—had been recorded some weeks before. The young woman was the lead singer of the band. This was the first time anyone had heard the tapes; they'd had to raise money to pay the recording studio first. She didn't have a record contract yet. She might never have one.

Her name was Sonja Pflug, her stage name was Catz Wailen. Everyone called her Catz now, even her family. Catz listened to the tape for two minutes, her lips gradually turning down at the ends, her forehead furrowing. She shifted on her stool. She couldn't seem to make herself comfortable, sitting in the recording studio, on the hard plastic stool. She was tense, and getting tenser. She listened to the tape, slowly shaking her head. She tapped on the glass separating the sound room from the control room, and the engineer switched off the tape. She flipped a toggle and spoke into the intercom.

"There's some kinda spoken voice in the background. Nothing we dubbed. Doesn't sound like anyone in the band. I can't quite make out what it's saying. What the hell *is* it? The voice . . . Wha's th' shrug supposed to mean, man? Huh? Come *on*. Uh—it must be CB radio or some shit, leaked in through the insulation. If, uh, if we're gonna keep it, y'know, outta the tapes, we damn well better identify it so we can screen it out. What frequency. What's that headshake supposed to—lissen, the air is fucking permeated with transmissions, radio and TV and microwave, and they're penetrating us all the time, secretly. . . . It's a kind of ether, like the old scientists use to say, a medium of whatever's commercially insipid. Right? So I figure we got a guy doing a moronic newscast or a spiel for beer mixed into our goddamn music. Look, I can *hear* it. It is real, yeah. So mix it—remix so I can hear it better, so I can figure out what it is, radio or what, maybe hear the call numbers. . . . This really screws the whole tape— Oh, okay? You got it audible? Okay . . . I . . ."

She replaced the earphones, signaling the engineer to roll the tape.

And the voice on the tape, heard clearly over the roar of the music now, said, "Hello, Catz." And then it laughed. A crazy sort of laugh. "I hope you can hear me clearly. The others here have had mixed success in making their voices heard in your world. The dead have no larynxes. At least, we don't from your viewpoint, because from your—" He stopped to laugh. The voice was always a little tinged with hysteria.

It was a familiar voice.

"—I'm sorry. Every time I think about viewpoint I have

to laugh, because of what's happened. How I see things now. And how I saw things then. Before the Big Sweep. Before I saw the big mind. The big mind is everybody's mind. But I have to get myself organized for you. I've been walking around—walking?—yeah, because I *do* have a body, in the *there* I'm at now. From your viewpoint I don't. Organization. I have to get myself in the right state of mind so I can tell you this story, because . . . I have to tell it from your world's—*heh*—viewpoint. I've been walking around thinking about it for days, drawing it together in my mind, going back to watch myself—back in Time, I mean: why hedge words?—to watch myself, uh, go through the whole sequence. To see it clearly. I've got plenty of time to see it clearly, because I'm clinging to your world for another forty relative years. I'm almost in your world, but not quite. Just a phase to one side. I'm clinging because of City, and the others. I'm helping them all. They're all interconnected, somewhere along the line. The overminds of each city going down to one vine in common . . . New York, San Francisco, Los Angeles—but L.A.'s so diffuse, fragmentary, predatory. . . . All the cities, all connected psychically. It's an ugly place and a beautiful place, that big mental reservoir. You're beautiful, Catz. I don't think I ever told you that. You're beautiful. I always wanted to tell you. I thought you'd laugh and say I was corny or blind. You'd have jeered at me. But now things are different. I can tell you I love you.

"And I can tell you why I did what I did. Why I let you go to Chicago—I knew you'd be in touch with the mind that's Chicago. On some level I knew what would happen all along. I'm filling a function now, Catz.

"Christ, Catz, you're beautiful. I can see right into you, your personal energy field, the focal point in that field where your—what did they call it?—your seat of consciousness is. I can see it glowing in you like an arc in a vacuum tube.

"I hope you can recognize my voice. I'm using a sort of psychokinesis to create the appropriate sound waves. I hope it sounds like me. It's a kind of interdimensional ventriloquism, I guess. You hear me? It's Stu! But who else, right?"

Catz took off the earphones. She signaled the engineer. He stopped the tape player. She sat staring, white-faced, at the control board. She stood up and went to her bag, took a medicine bottle from it. She took a calmer, and a deep breath. *It's really him,* she thought.

She went back to her seat and reached for the earphones. She replaced them on her head. She hesitated. She sat still for a minute, convincing herself to go on with it. She signaled the engineer, and listened.

"I want you to understand me, Catz. Why I couldn't go with you. Why I had to let City do what he did.

"It's funny, but time means nothing to me now. Once you learn the maze, you can travel either way. We can stand apart and look at ourselves being born. I've stood, invisible, by my mother's hospital bed, and watched myself being born! I watched myself grow up. I went back to witness it all again. To rewitness, see things objectively. I'm going to tell you the story, though you were there for most of it. I hope I can get it all on your tape. I'm going to start with that night in the club, that second night of your San Francisco tour. You'd just got back from Chicago. The night I asked you to psi the guy I wanted to hire for a bouncer. I'm going into the necessary mindstate now. I can feel it. Third person. I'm the third person, all right."

He laughed. Catz winced. Just a little crazy.

"It was about the tenth of May, 2008. In good ol' San Francisco . . . what San Francisco was then, before the changes, The Sweep, and—never mind. It's funny—not long ago, relative to my personal sense of time, I stood in the midst of an explosion. Part of The Sweep. A house blew up around me. It didn't hurt me. I enjoyed it. I walked away from there as if I'd just come from bathing in a turbulent sea.

"I'm organized now. I'm going back. Ellis Street. Club Anesthesia. *My* club, no matter what they said about it. The *Chronicle* rated it, '. . . one star if you're looking for an esthetic and humane atmosphere, four stars if you're looking for endless noise, fistfights, eccentrics, hookers, and muggings.' *Fuck* the *Chronicle*. It was my club, and I loved it. . . ."

Catz listened, feeling as if she were melting inside. Sweat beaded on her forehead. In the background, behind the disembodied voice, her band wailed and throbbed and roared *angst rock,* metal stripped down, fast and angry music like the echo of a subway thundering into the station.

The voice on the tape told a story.

WUN!

IT WAS SATURDAY NIGHT, ten o'clock, which means that the club was full to capacity. It wasn't just full, it was tumescent. They were spilling out the windows. That was fine with Stuart Cole. The club depended on the extra revenue brought in by that Saturday night excess. But it meant he had to hire and, worse, pay three, count 'em, three bouncers for that one night. And Cole had only found one bouncer, already overworked, the poor fellow's knuckles bruised. Cole was looking for two more and had already been turned down by two black belts, an ex-Green Beret, and a bulldyke. It seemed they wanted to keep their faces intact. The Anesthesia had a reputation.

Cole was mixing a Rusty Nail and thinking bouncers when he noticed the man in the mirror sunglasses. He noticed the man as the eye goes to a buoy before the waves, because of the buoy's immobility: a solid thing in liquid flux. Crowds are liquid, full of currents and eddies. People are soft things, mostly water, and when they move there is more flow than jerkiness. But this man moved like an ice-breaker—hard and implacable, but with its own singleminded grace. He was not massive, or stiff, but there was an air of inflexibility about him. Permanence.

The ideal bouncer.

Appraising the man, Cole decided he wasn't affluent: the stranger's long black trenchcoat was torn in two places and missing the belt and the brown broad-brimmed hat pulled low over his face was losing its shape. The mirror sunglasses looked new and they caught the whirling reflection of the old-fashioned mirrorfacet ball over the dancefloor. *Maybe an undercover cop,* Cole thought. Or worse, maybe a vigilante. The vigs had been threatening to clean the prostitutes out with more vigstyle hit-and-run specials, and the club had its share of hookers.

He had a square face, pale and unblemished, but rough, like a marble cornerstone eroded to resemble a man. His jutting cleft chin stuck out farther than his pug nose. His hair was short, curly, with a blue-black metallic sheen. He was five-seven, medium build. But there was complacent formidability in the skyscraper uprightness of his stance.

Cole watched him, thinking: *Be careful who you hire . . .* In San Francisco one didn't take chances with just any maniac off the street; it had to be the *right* sort of maniac.

So Cole watched the man without seeming to. He gave over mixing drinks to Bill Wallach and pretended he wanted to check out the stage equipment. He could get a better look from the stage.

So straightening mike-stands and needlessly adjusting lead-wires, Cole watched. The mirror-eyed man was standing in the shadows by the cigarette machine, on the edge of the mob, impassively observing. Cole wished he could see his eyes. But Cole's gaze kept returning to the man's lips. His lips were colorless, compressed, recessed, and—they didn't move. Not a twitch. Catz came onto the stage to ask if the equipment were all right, and why was Cole fumbling

with a guitar strap . . . ? "I'm, uh, ad*justing* it, Catz. Hey—
do you think you could keep your eye on the guy by the cigarette machine? In the mirrorshades. He's either dangerous or he's the perfect bouncer. Either way I want to know.
I don't want to approach him about a job till I know he's
cool, I don't need any goddamn vig infiltrators. . . ."

Catz shrugged and nodded, her short silver-stained hair
bouncing like a foil curtain fringe around her wolfish face;
her golden eyes narrowed the way they did when she was
about to ask a question. Cole shook his head at her and
went back to the bar to wait for The Catz Report.

Catz's band joined her on the stage and when they got
their instruments tuned and strapped on and plugged in,
Cole hit the switch that cut the disco tape and shouted into
the bar-mike: "Lewdies and genitalmen—CATZ WAILEN!"
Half the people on the dance floor groaned and the other
half cheered. All murmured expectantly. Even those who
didn't like Catz had heard stories about her.

Tuning her guitar, Catz bent and whispered something
to a cocktail waitress, who nodded and threaded her way
through pawing hands to Cole.

"Catz says to tell you her 'report is in the song lyrics.' So
what the hell is she talking about?"

"Tell you later," Cole answered, though he had no intention of telling her later. So she filled her tray with drinks
and went to slop the hogs and Cole waited. *The report's in the
lyrics?* He shivered. He was one of the few people who could
make out the words to Catz's lyrics. Because he'd known her
for years? Perhaps. But also because there was an affinity
between them. Most people didn't know that Catz improvised her lyrics. Spontaneously composed them. They were
different every night. Sometimes they even rhymed.

The band was attuned, tuned, plugged in, and waiting.
It was a five-piece *angst rock* band, with Catz the focalpiece.

She blinked when the stage lights came on, then she tapped the microphone to see if it were alive, and barked at the audience: "SHUDDUP!"

Catz was the only performer Cole had ever seen who could get results that way.

The crowd was particularly noisy that night, breaking glasses and throwing the rubber bottles and laughing and shrieking. It escalated all night; by midnight the crowd would revel in its own thunder, an uproar that would shake the walls. Except—Catz, a thin, gangly longnecked little woman, had said *shut up*.

And they shut up.

It was miraculous: It was quiet. A few coughs, a snicker, the clicks of cigarette lighters. The smokefilled room flared here and there as joints were lit in anticipation of the live music. The crowd on the dance floor poised itself, flexing, waiting to spring into the song rhythms.

The quiet was unnatural and everyone waited for it to end. That expectation was more than satisfied when the band slashed into its opening set. There was an explosion of fuzz and feedback and the lead guitar running through a fierce opening solo that sounded like an unoiled winch squealing as it strained to lift a ton of loose scrapmetal.

The thunder of the bass tied the heavy-metal grind into a single charging unit, as bolts hold together a speeding army tank. Catz put aside her rhythm guitar and began to sing. Cole, frowning, decoded her screech:

All you cheap suckers and all you cheap slutters
are obsolete you are obsolete
all you whining women and all you drooling men
all you hustlers with fraud your only friend
you are obsolete, you're obsolete
no more room for you on the street

you jerks are obsolete
'Cuz the street is tired of taking it, the street is tired o' you
it's sick of getting pissed on and sick o' Cadillacs
night becomes white & day becomes black
when the city come a-walkin'
city comes walkin' to claim its own . . .

The lead guitar took a long solo, defining youth in the language of electricity. Catz danced in a hundred permutations of the moth's last spasm as it burns in candleflame. Catz kicked the bassplayer in the ass and laughed and pinwheeled her arms and jumped four feet in the air, spun, kicked the lead guitar on the way down, slapped knees, clapped her hands, landed square on the stage, snaked her neck, shook her ass and shoulders in double provocation, and never missed the beat.

The drums and bass quieted in dramatic preface and her overlarge golden eyes got bigger yet, her pixiecut platinum hair clung to her head with sweat. Her face lost all uncertainty and she nodded at the man in the mirror sunglasses; she sang:

City come a-walkin' to claim its own
Hindus and their avatars
Catz and her guitars
Zeus swanning Leda
sometimes the world takes the shape of gods
sometimes the gods take the form of men
sometimes the gods walk the earth like mortal men
And tonight the city come a-walkin'
and we're all obsolete . . .

Catz shrieked it not quite on key and barely in time to the music and the crowd had no idea what she was saying.

But they loved it. Because she made them feel that whatever it was she was singing, she *meant* it.

The song escalated, as wars do, the mirrorfacet ball turned and threw shards of light, rubber bottles whistled by, smoke unfurled, and Catz looked hard at Cole (and Cole wished he were not forty-two and getting paunchy) and she spoke into the mike: "This part of the song—hey, you slutters, are you *LISTENIN*—" The crowd shouted back in happy fury. "All right! Slutterkids, this part of the song tells a story in ten parts, like ten chapters in a book. I'll name off each chapter and you gotta figure for yourself what's happening by visualizing the music's invisible architecture (if you dumbshits folla me), so FUCKING PAY ATTEN*SHUNNN*!" She took a deep breath, the band paused, the crowd noise lulled, and she sang out:

"WUN!" The lead guitar strangles a writhing riffsnake and Cole seems to see himself and the man with the mirror sunglasses together on the street.

"—TEW!" The bass comes in hard and fabricates images of the mirror-eyed man on a TV screen.

"thuh-*REE!*" The drums shape an image of vigilantes firing at random into a rockshow crowd.

"FOH-ur!" The synthesizer trembles their cortexes with sub- and ultrasonic sound images, images of Catz and Cole bleeding on a wooden floor, surrounded by laughing men.

"FIGH-uhv!" Rhythm guitar brings a vision of Cole and Catz making love.

"uh-*SIXZZ!*" The base, working with the lead, contrasts light and shade to sketch out Cole, lying on a bed; beside him Catz is packing a suitcase.

"SEV-uhn!" Drums evoke an image of Cole stepping back as a close friend slams a door in his face.

"A-A-ate!" The keyboards show Cole a snapshot of himself hustled into a jail cell.

"*NYE*-uhn!" Cole sees himself standing naked before a mirror, rubbing at his eyes.

"*TENNN!*" All instruments merge into a single chord calling up a vision of Cole suspended in the midst of an explosion. . . .

Abruptly, the song ended. Cole had to run to the bathroom.

He felt somewhat better after he'd thrown up. He mixed himself a drink to fade the lingering disorientation. *Why did she show me those things?*

Cole returned to the bar and began to work, as a sort of yoga for calmness. Catz kicked the band into another tune.

The stranger in the mirror sunglasses watched the stage pensively—he was the only man in the room not moving to the music. Even the bartenders tapped their fingers. But the stranger simply stared. And didn't move.

Cole tended bar, feeding the insatiable multimouthed monster kept barely at bay by the wooden counter—he poured drinks down its throat and its mouths clamored for more. . . . At regular intervals along the bar Interfund units accepted cards handed over by buyers, showed whether the cardholder had funds in his or her account, instantaneously transferred the money from the account of the holder to that of the recipient, verified the transaction with its digital number display panel. . . .

As happened at least once a night, someone plunked cash money down on the counter instead of an Interfund card. It was an old man with a mane of dirty white hair and rheumy blue eyes. "Where's your money, Granpy?" Cole said. "Real money, I mean. ITF card."

"Goddamnit, *this here's* real money, fuggin cardshit's the phoney stuff—"

"Yeah yeah, I know how you feel, but we sell nothing for cash, slutter, nobody does anymore. Not even beernuts.

Everything—coffee or liquor, whatever—you gotta have an ITF card. . . . I don't know how you people get by, using that stuff; there must be only three stores left in the city using cash money. Instantaneous Transfer of Funds—"

"FUGGIT!" snarled the old man, licking dry lips, scooping up his money. "Music in here stinks anyway!"

He left. "Sorry Granpy!" Cole called after him sadly. *Some of them just can't adjust.*

The rest of Catz's set seemed to flash by, so busy was Cole. Catz announced a break and summarily left the stage. Cole flipped the disco back on and mixed Catz a drink. She sucked down her double dry martini in one gasping gulp and Cole served her two more. Catz was hyperactive, trembling—as always after a set, worked up to a fever pitch.

"Did you hear?" she asked.

Cole leaned across the bar, planted his elbows on the wood and his chin on his hands and asked, "What the hell am I supposed to make out of that?"

"I thought you specialized in poetry in *college,* Stu," she said, half-mocking.

"So? I want a report on whether I can trust a guy to be a bouncer and you give me 'tonight the city comes walking' or some such shit."

"Did you get the psi-shots I sent you?"

"Yeah but—I didn't really understand them."

"Well—me either. You wanna know if you can trust the guy?" she laughed. " 'A guy' you call him. 'Trust him' you say. Christ! Yeah, you could trust that guy to babysit your kids if you had some or hold all your money for you or to bounce for you. If he agreed to do it, he'd do it. Only, he wouldn't agree to it. He's got no time for it—he's got things to do and only one night to do them in. . . . Anyway, that's no *one* person. Don't you understand that? *That's the City.* Itself. The sleeping part, awake and dreaming corporeally, slutterkid. Y'know? It's the gestalt of the whole place, this whole fuckin' city, rolled up in one man. Sometimes the world takes the shape of gods and those gods take the form of men. Sometimes. This time. That's a whole city, that man, and I *don't* mean that metaphorically."

She said it straight-faced. If anyone else had said it, Cole would have rolled his eyes. No one can look at a stranger once and know him as if she'd spent a lifetime with him. No one except Catz. Catz had gifts. A man from Duke University had once offered her big money to come back east and submit to esper tests. But Catz refused. Catz sees only when she chooses, when intuition tells her the time is right. So Cole knew Catz's judgment could be trusted—it was the judgment of her gift. And so Cole knew who the stranger was. And was afraid.

Catz went back to the stage. Suddenly it seemed very stuffy in the Club Anesthesia. Dope smoke and cigarette smog and the myriad human reeks were constricting Cole's throat; he was nearly gagging. He told Bill to take over, and went outside.

He stood on the sidewalk and breathed the crisp spring night.

Cole couldn't stand still; excess energy paced him back and forth in front of the club.

He hadn't come out there just for air. He'd come to make certain of something.

He looked at the city.

The traffic was high, mostly tricks sniffing for quick-credit pussy, and teenage cruisers. The cars honked and growled, headlights fenced, kids shouted incoherencies out car windows. Someone casually pitched a bottle at Cole; it bounced off the brick wall to his right. "Assholes," he muttered absentmindedly. The concrete reefs were strati-fied with lights—dim blue lights of televisions in darkened living rooms, bright white lights of bathrooms, multicolored lights from parties. Pornies leered in pink neon and a subtle breeze played idly with dirty confetti in the gutter.

"Brother, I wonder could you help me out—"

Cole glanced at the wino, took two steps to the corner ITF booth and punched out two dollars. The wino's own greasy card—any card next inserted—would now stand him to a pint of wine.

The wino credited the two bucks and tottered off. Cole thrust his hands in his trouser pockets and scowled. His apron flapped in the breeze. He could smell exhaust fumes and stale wine and staler pizzas from the three-fifty-a-slice place on the corner. The sidewalk was busy with hookers, a few plasheen punks, sparecrediters, and one woman walking her poodle while keeping a hand in her purse, probably on a gun.

The disco was still pounding from the club. Catz hadn't started her second set. He smiled, remembering the arguments he'd had with her about disco. She'd say it was all computer made now, based on personality polling, psychological trend profiles, and that made it uniform to whatever was the status quo which, in the end, revealed disco to be a tool of repression, a soothing social sedative that helped reaffirm things-as-they-are. The establishment's rock'n'roll. And Cole would laugh and reply that all popular music reflected the status quo or the yearning to be a part of it, and he ran his club according to the preference of his customers as much as possible—he had the waitresses poll them twice a year, asking things like what kind of music they'd like to hear between live sets, and mostly they wanted disco. That made it possible for Cole to occasionally hire unusual bands, radical bands like Catz Wailen—because he compromised in other areas. And because most of the bands he hired were conventional bar bands, singing whatever was in vogue. But Catz would snarl that he was pandering to the fascist mentality and she'd add, "In the final analysis, Cole-my-man, you're a collectivist. You're a whore for the will of the people. I'm an individualist." And Cole would object and the argument would go round and round, like disco.

The disco was cut off when Catz shrieked over the microphone—the P.A. amplification of her voice resounding up and down the street, making the hookers laugh and the loafers start—"Shut that brainless Muzak OFF!"

Catz's music rang onto the street, shaking the lampposts—Cole had his hand against one, he could feel the bass vibrating in the steel column. Feeling a need to retreat from the noise for a while, and to escape from a flavor of accusation in Catz's singing that tonight seemed subtly directed at him. Cole strolled away from the club. Hands in his pockets he walked south, stopping now and then to bullshit with the dealers and the guys hanging out, making big futile talk under the lamps . . . Cole nodding and saying, "Zat right? Sounds good, if you can swing the capital," when Mario told him he was going to get "Big Cred" in fashions because his old lady had come up with these backless jeans, seethrough fabric over the buttocks, that he was going to find an investor and really *clean debit*. And Cole said, "You always did like to watch ass, Mario." The others laughed—Filipinos down from Mission Street looking for action. Cole handed out a few cigarettes, and declined Mario's offer to let him back his hot fashion killing, and pretended to take a toke on someone's 'loid stick, and went his way.

He talked to the black clubfoot at the hardcore tri-vid store, politely looking at the latest live-action viewers, glancing at the display racks with mild interest, the figures all merging into fleshy knots in the multiplicity of human coupling. Thinking about it, he suspected he was visiting the porn clerk because he was hoping to find a little arousal, maybe just a twinge, glancing at the holographic fertility rites. Just checking in with himself, to see if things had changed yet. But no, no arousal, not even half an erection. ... He laughed, politely, at the heap of old books the clerk, chuckling, showed him in the back room. No one read the porn novels anymore. It was all magazines and tri-vid and movies and multi-stimulators. "I'm keepuh the slutterin things in here for five yeuh now, thinkin I'm sell the bassuds," said the clerk, stumping back to the main room. "Fuggitall. I'ma burn the bassuds tuh keep warm if they shut off my fuel this yeuh. Fuel rationing a mothuhfuckuh."

Cole agreed and went back to the streets. He passed a group of three black hookers; the one who didn't know him made the obligatory offer, "You wanna date?" The other two pretended to come onto him, for a joke, and Cole pretended to be interested. "But you don't charge enough, ladies. For fine leg like that I pay no less than $737,000 creds. But I couldn't do that to you. The IRS boys'd take you apart."

"Shit, I do it for a free drink in that rat-hole of yours, Cole."

"You don't get a drink inna rat-hole, bitch."

"I meant that fine public drinking establishment you run, baby."

"Baby, huh? Fine public drinking establishment, huh? You come around at midnight I give you a brandy and Seven for that."

The others quickly pretended to praise his club, "I read about that sucker in *Bon Appetit*. Hey but I *did* see your picture inna magazine for real, man."

"What?"

"In *Overview,* man."

"Yeah, she's always readin' some shit," said one of the others, lighting a joint.

"An article about what a all-around guy you was, Cole man. You said some stuff in there's gonna piss off some vigilante assholes."

"Like *what?* I don't remember. The guy asked me questions and I answered them and then I forgot about it. I shouldn't uh let 'em interview me."

"You said the vigs were working for the local hard guys who wanted to organize the hookers and th' hookers union wouldn't let 'em so they hired these guys to harass the hookers an' the hustlers, coverin' up by acting like they morally outraged but all they want's protection cred . . ."

"Right fucking *on,*" said someone, Cole didn't notice who. He was occupied with worrying. The vigs had firebombed a club in Oakland for allowing hookers inside. . . .

Cole said, "I'll see you ladies later," and walked on, kicking through the refuse of an overturned trash can. A cockroach big as a mouse ran over the toe of his boot; he kicked the insect angrily away, and it rebounded from the windshield of a parked Mini-Cad steamcar.

He went to a combination phone booth and news kiosk, sat on the metal stool, inserted his ITF card in the slot, and punched the code for magazines. The directory of available magazines appeared on the vid screen over the phone. He selected *Overview,* May 2008. The magazine's contents page appeared; he punched the specific page:

THREE MEN AND THREE NIGHTCLUBS

I took three nights and talked to three club owners, and I got three different facets of one city. Friday, it was Billy Russiter, owner of the swank Carlton on . . .

Cole grimaced and pressed the fastforward button until he found the section dealing with the Club Anesthesia.

> . . . Stuart Cole's peculiar sense of humor is first apparent in the name of the club, and then the club's decor. All of us, of course, go to bars for anesthesia, to dampen pain with alcohol and the distraction of a show, a chance to get lost in a crowd. The club is—or was, before most of the furniture was broken up, the decorations vandalized— painted and furnished to resemble a hospital ward. The middle row of tables is made up of hospital single-beds whose mattresses have been replaced by tabletops; here and there stand I.V. bottle racks, medicine cabinets, patient progress charts on the walls. But of course much of this effect, and the offwhite wall color, is lost when the lights go down and the band on the small stage revs up.
>
> Stu Cole is a middle-aged man, perhaps younger than he looks, aged with hard times and a variety of hard jobs. His hair is thinning and his benign expression doesn't conceal permanent worrylines.

Cole scowled and skipped quickly ahead to the interview.

> *Overview:* You came out here from New York City ten years ago?
>
> *Cole:* New York is where I'd lived for eight years, yes. But I'm a native of the bay area. I grew up mostly in Oakland and Berkeley. I've got a strong affinity for the area. I used to have dreams about San Francisco—vivid dreams!—even after I'd been in New York six years. Maybe that's one reason I came back.
>
> *Overview:* What did you do when you were in New York?
>
> *Cole:* That's too general a question. If you mean, how did I live, I guess . . . well, I started out as a hustler.
>
> *Overview:* A male prostitute?
>
> *Cole:* Sure. You wanted this to be a candid interview, right? It was mostly with gay older men, but some hetero couples, too. I wasn't particularly gay, but I could function

that way when it paid me. It was a bad scene though. I gave it up when some creep left me way out in Queens in a railroad yard in the rain. He just shoved me out of his car as I was getting dressed again. I applied for grants, got back into school.

Overview: And you graduated with honors, I understand, but you refused your degree. Why?

Cole: I felt that degrees were elitist, and meaningless except to set you apart from Everyman. I didn't want to be set apart from Everyman. I've always felt sort of . . . uh, alienated, I guess, from people, and that's made me want to belong all the more. So I guess I—I looked all my life for a situation where I could feel I belonged. I needed some kind of family. I was never close to my parents. My sister's been missing for a long time. So all I've got is my Club and my . . . well, the whole damn *city* really.

Overview: It's odd how San Francisco's fulltime residents have such a strong sense of home in their city; some of them are fanatics about it.

Cole: I guess I am too. A fanatic—but not in the love-it-or-leave-it sense. A great many people get upset about the town being overrun with tourists. To me tourists are part of the furnishings. The town depends on them. This is a unique city in some ways because it's so compressed. I mean, it's all crowded—the main part of it—onto this little peninsula, and up and down these steep hills. That means that the Latin communities and the black communities and the Filipinos and the Chinese and the Japanese and the gays, gays everywhere, and the Arabs and East Indian and the middleclass whites—they're all rubbing shoulders all the time, various "ghettos" overlapping. So there's a strong feeling of community, I think.

Overview: I sense a certain tension in your style of talking, Stu. You sort of vacillate between street talk and the speeching of an educated man . . .

Cole: (laughing) Well, there's education and there's education. I've found the street education to be more useful.

But yeah, I guess I'm a funny mix. I've known a lot of
what the newspapers call "underworld" people, and a
lot of artists and photographers. . . . I guess I'm always
reaching for a full sense of this city. All the different
parts of it. I suppose in taking out all the loans, going up
to my ass in debt to get the club off the ground ten years
ago, I was trying to find a neutral ground for contact
with the city as a whole. For a while the club was decorated like all the others. But I needed a change. You'd
be surprised at the number of different kinds of people
we get in here. Voguers, neopunks, transexers, artists,
mechanics, some of the straightest people you'll ever
see and some of the most offbeat. . . .

Overview: But you're trying for that, it seems to me, with
your programming. Multimedia shows, standup come-
dians, soul bands, rock bands, jazz bands, top forty copy
bands . . . And now Catz Wailen . . .

Cole: Well, I've known Catz for a long time. There has to be
someone like her come around at the beginning of
every decade. To clear the air. In the sixties it was Bob
Dylan and Lou Reed and Hendrix, in the seventies Patti
Smith, in the eighties John Lydon . . .

Overview: That's putting her in illustrious company.

"You snotty bastard," Cole murmured. He forced himself to
read on.

Cole: She deserves to be in that company, man. She—

Overview: You were involved in city politics a few years back,
and then you went low profile.

Cole: Oh, I wrote some petitions, circulated them, got some
referendums rolling, wrote a few articles, backed a can-
didate . . . Not much . . .

Overview: Still, there were rumors you were going to run for
commissioner.

Cole: I considered it. I decided that my chances weren't
good. But sure, I guess I'm concerned with city politics,
and the administration of the city, things beyond enter-
tainment industry concerns, yeah. I identify with the

place, I guess. So its problems are my problems.

Overview: You raised some hackles, though, when you tried to get a vote on allowing small businesses to continue using cash.

Cole: All that BED lobbying has people scared.

Overview: What are they scared of?

Cole: The power of the organization. It's got the reins on all of us because it controls our means of doing business. It's a dangerous situation. Suppose organized crime—just for an example—got control of ITF through BED. Since all transactions are done electronically and since you can control electronics from a distance, they could embezzle or . . . well, I don't think I should get into that.

Overview: I understand yours is one of the clubs that got a warning from the vigilantes.

Cole: Yes. They pasted it on the door. Took me two hours to get it off. But they're wrong—I haven't been "condoning" prostitution. I haven't been condemning it either. People are people, they'll always use prostitutes. Now that it's semi-legal, like potsmoking, with its own union, things are safer for everybody. This new puritanism is absurd, man. It's suspect.

Overview: What do you mean suspect?

Cole: I mean these guys are too well organized. They're hitting the vices that make big money—gambling, prostitution—but they're not attacking the new government-subsidy drug programs, free smack to junkies, free speed to speedfreaks to keep them all in hand. I think they work for someone who's making money off vice and wants to make more. . . .

The screen went blank except for the words DEPOSIT ITF CRED $1 FOR ADDITIONAL TEN MINUTES. Cole shrugged and left the booth. He walked back toward the club, thinking. The noise of taverns rose and fell as he passed them.

It was a softly warm night. He approached the Anesthesia. Catz's amplified voice echoed off the buildings around him He thought about the psi-flashes she'd sent him. Something cold walked his spine.

He paused outside the door of the club as Catz's band fell silent so that she could recite one of her poems. Cole listened to the city, sifting noises. He watched, sorting impressions. What he was looking for was there. It was the presence of the city, the gestalt overpattern uniting its diversity, the invisible relationship between the broken glass in the gutter and the antenna on the limousine, the connection unseen between the odor of vomited wine and the scent of open-air florist shops . . . the presence that only a fool won't look for. Because, sensitizing to that presence, you usually knew if there was a lethal gang around the corner or if a fire was about to break out in your tenement. You found yourself leaving a place suddenly, without knowing why—until you read about it the next day in the papers. And that presence was there now. But if the stranger was who Catz claimed he was . . .

Then Cole understood. The presence was there, outside. But the personality, the sense of willful intelligence supporting the hum of city activity—that was nearly muted. It was localized. It was dim out here on the street. Because the city's personality was indoors, embodied in a man waiting in Cole's club. Indoors, and wearing a battered brown hat and mirror sunglasses.

Cole nodded to himself.

I was trying to find a neutral ground for contact with the city as a whole. . . .

Cole went into his club.

There he was. Cole had no trouble locating the mirror-eyed man.

Catz was talking to him, up close as if he were an old friend. Cole pushed through the crowd, eyes fixed on the stranger. He wanted badly to speak with him; he had no idea what he would say.

30

Cole stopped three feet away, looking at his reflection, twinned in the mirror sunglasses. Catz was talking in a quiet voice, speaking close to the man's ear; the endless chant of disco formulas mazed Catz's voice from Cole. A dozen questions jumped into Cole's mind. All of them seemed imbecilic. But he wanted to ask, 'City, where have you hidden my sister Pearl? She's an alcoholic and I haven't seen her in eight months. I think she's either dead or somewhere in Oakland. Oakland's not death but it's definitely a coma.' And 'City, isn't there a better place I can live than a two-room apartment in the Mission district?' And 'City, why did my best friend have to die on the freeway under the wheels of a semitruck? Do you have something against hitchhikers?' But Cole said none of those things. He stared into the mirrorshades and felt unreasonably like crying. He took off his apron and tossed it on the floor. He was done with it for the night.

A cocktail waitress spoke to City. The disco softened for a moment and Cole heard: "The people at table five would like to buy you a drink, sir." City nodded and followed her through the forest of plasheen coats and convictskin leggings, toward table five where sat a blank-faced group of voguers waiting, hoping desperately for a laugh. They were dressed in translucent woven-plastic suits with hems tricked out in soft blue and red neon.

City was forty feet from the four voguers; as Cole watched, City was momentarily lost in the crowd. He had gone into the thick of the mob wearing his hat and worn trenchcoat; he came into view ten seconds later wearing a glittering metalmesh vest, translucent woven-plastic suit jacket, yellow satin leggings, no hat, spiked convictskin boots (Negro)—and the same black metalframe mirrorshades.

Catz had been right. A city walked among men.

Catz stood in the background, listening as City talked to the group at the table. Cole couldn't see City's face but he could tell by the looks of horrified fascination on the four uppercrusts that he was speaking to them. Catz was laughing. Cole made his way toward the table; the closer he got, the louder the disco music became, though he was getting farther from the speakers. . . .

Ordinarily, when he worked the bar, he didn't hear the disco from the six-foot speakers ringing the dancefloor. He'd learned to screen it out. A man paying close attention to the same disco songs running in a ninety-minute tape loop will become hysterical or comatose. The machine perfection of incessant rhythm, the emotionless invocation to emotions, the hypnotic inexorability of a thousand variations of bump-and-grind—the labyrinthine stuff of paranoia.

But right then, Cole was listening. The music brought him closer to City.

The closer he got to table five, the voguers now standing and shouting, the louder the music rang in his ears, the taped singer chanting: MAKE IT GO ROUND AND DON'T LET IT STOP/LISTEN TO THE MAN WHET THE RAZOR ON THE STROP/MAKE IT GO ROUND AND DON'T LET IT STOP/LISTEN TO THE SOUND WHET THE RAZOR ON THE STROP/MAKE IT GO ROUND . . .

Those were the only lyrics, computer-composed like the music, and they repeated till the song's fade-out.

He reached the table. City had finished talking to them. Now he was watching as one of the studied voguers drew a needledagger from a knee-high convictskin boot and introduced it to another shimmering voguer's glittering ribs. The recipient of this cold and attenuated gift trembled and bawled and fell back, tripping over another voguer who was apparently attempting to rape the knife-wielder's wife; the woman was beating the rapist over the head and shoulders with a rubber bottle. Catz and the crowd watched, chuckling. Looking faintly annoyed, Rich the bouncer broke it up, hauled the bodies outdoors.

City turned to Cole. City no longer wore plasheen regalia; now he wore a black suit, white shirt, and blue spiral-tie—like Cole. City set off for the door. Cole followed without questioning, not questioning even for an instant. Catz signaled her band to finish the night with an instrumental jam, and she came along.

When City stepped out onto the sidewalk a five-car wreck took place, as if the traffic humbled itself for him in a genuflection of crumpling metal. A shred of chrome bumper whipped past Cole's head and buried itself in the brick wall. The night was fierce with the electricity of urban tension. City glanced at the car wreck, nodded, turned away. Stepping over the voguers still thrashing and bleeding on the sidewalk, Catz and Cole followed City, just behind and to his left, watching him from the corners of their eyes.

Behind, a blue gasohol Ford *Stomper* pickup, a yellow electric VW *Thug,* a golden '69 Ford Falcon, a white steam-powered Lincoln Continental, and a red VW bug were enmeshed by crumpled snouts, married from five directions; a pentagram described in twisted steel, shredded rubber, flaring gasoline, shard glass, and flesh oozing red.

Accompanying City down the street, seeming to radiate from his torso: the disco tape-loop. Singleminded, incessant, an audio blueprint of an urban street-plan.

The computer-composed music echoed from brick walls and rattled store windows and brought a sigh from Cole. Catz whistled along with it, skipping jauntily and kicking at garbage cans.

Cole whispered to Catz who was humming and zipping up her black leather jacket. "What did he say to the voguers that made them jump each other?"

She laughed. "He told the man with the knife about sex his best friend—the one he stabbed—had with his wife; the man with the knife stuck his best friend because his friend was his lover and I gathered he was not supposed to have been fooling around with any but *him,* and in fucking the knifer's wife he'd been unfaithful to the knifer."

"I get the idea. What about the rapist?"

"The rapist was the victim's brother. All his life he'd desired his sister; City explained to him that his sister had had relations with his older brother but was disgusted by *him,* and that she led him on and enjoyed seeing that he wanted her but would never let him touch her."

"And they knew it was the truth. And they never doubted his word."

"No, they never doubted. He's as inarguable as a Mack truck doing eighty. Do *you* doubt him?"

"No. I'm here, aren't I? But where are we going? Why is he here tonight? Why did he come among us? And how?"

"He wants to know himself from the inside out. A natural enough motivation. He is prodding himself, testing reflexes, investigating, tasting, and vindicating. How? Collective unconscious possessed and transmuted a man. He makes it *true,* he resolves tensions, he justifies the dramas of lives by bringing destinies to consummation."

"You're being enigmatic just to torment me. You enjoy seeing me confused, Catz."

" 'Pleased tuh meet you, hope you guessed my name/ confusin' you is the nature of my game.' "

It was the heart of Saturday night. The crowds were bent on private destinations and they saw only those destinations in their minds' eyes, and not much else; destinations like carrots before donkeys. So they didn't notice that though City radiated disco, he carried no radio or tape deck.

In the distance the severe lineaments of the street converged in a patina of glamorous scales, refractions of neon lights, headlights, streetlights, and metal; glints diffused through a cloud of cigarette smoke, steam from manholes, and carbon monoxide.

The warm breeze mixed odors of cooked meat and garbage. Cole felt ill.

And he was nervous. The city seemed unnaturally vivid to his eyes; the sounds of it, boys whistling, pistons gnashing, gears clashing—too loud.

Headache and nausea collaborated to steep him in misery. More than anything, Cole wanted the abysmal disco to stop. But it never occurred to him to leave City's side.

They were heading up through Chinatown and half the signs had become ideograms, enigmas in neon; the hill got steeper, Cole's headache pounded harder. At the crest of the hill they paused to admire the skyline. The angular graph of citylights was reflected in City's mirror eyes and his mouth opened slightly as he breathed some inaudible name.

Boyish laughter echoed from the left. City turned that way, onto a dark side street; garbage was piled on the sidewalk beside the back doors of Chinese groceries, a stench of fish and vegetables gone bad.

They walked rapidly, silently, for fifteen blocks, until presently they passed out of Chinatown and were half-skidding down a steep hill through a residential district of high and haughty Victorian houses squeezed close to one another.

Abruptly City halted and turned to contemplate the houses on the left. The disco redundancies quieted to a whisper.

The front doors burst open on three adjacent houses. From these rushed five people, a couple each from the nearest houses and one old woman from the farther. Faces florid, they dashed down their wooden stairs and curved agate-walks to where City, Cole, and Catz waited beneath a streetlight. Cole glanced at City. He stared. City now wore a conservative grey suit, polished, expensive-looking brown shoes.

The couples were early middle-age and upper middle-class. A man and wife with squarish German faces and tightly clipped grey-black hair; the man wore a black string-tie half undone which he now self-consciously retied. The other couple were in pajamas and robes, the man balding and portly, his mouth gaping beneath his mustache, his slippered feet skittering nervously over the sidewalk; his wife peered at City through thick glasses; her mouse-brown hair caught up in a hairnet. The fifth person, an old woman, wore a white nightgown, a threadbare blue bathrobe, slippers, and a hairnet bristling with red plastic roses. She carried a flashlight in her right hand, a small nickel-plated pistol in her left. Her dark-ringed eyes were black, the lines about them were bitter. She spoke first:

"What's the emergency anyway?" She turned to peer up at her house as if expecting to see flames. "I heard—" She frowned.

The other robed woman spoke tremulously, "What did *you* hear? We heard someone shouting 'Emergency! Get out into street!' So goddamn loud I thought my eardrums would break. My God, I thought it was a Civil Defense alert—"

"Yes, yes, that's what we heard too," said the old man with the faint German accent. "It was official voice. 'Emergency! Out into the street!' " They turned to glare at City, waiting for an explanation.

"Do you want to see your children tonight?" It was the first time Cole had heard City speak. A cold but resonant voice. City's face had changed again. Same strong jaw, but

now his nose was hooked, his lips pressed into the queru-
lous squiggle of a bureaucrat of some authority. Same
opaque glasses. His manner was brisk and official when he
reached into his jacket pocket and extracted a long black
wallet which he flipped open to display a SFPD badge. Vice
Squad.

"Our . . . children?" The old woman asked, trying to conceal her eagerness.

"Yes. If you come now. Leave the gun and flashlight in
your mailbox and come now."

"Now? This time of night?" Demanded the matron in the
black gown.

City nodded. He pointed at the street behind them.

Cole turned and was startled by the two cabs, waiting with
headlights brilliant and doors hanging open. He hadn't
heard them drive up.

The faces of both cab drivers were in shadow.

There was no further argument. Everyone got into the
cabs. The old woman rode in Cole's, the front seat. The couples rode in the cab behind. The disco music from City,
jammed in beside Cole, was soft and distant. Cole suspected
that the old woman couldn't hear it at all.

Catz sat on City's right. City crowded Cole against the
door. Cole's arm was forced up against City's side—a side
that was hard and cold as granite. City's elbow, lying half on
Cole's hip, pinched with the weight of a bar of iron. City sat
inert, staring ahead. For the first time Cole could see City's
sunglasses up close.

The stems of the sunglasses did not rest on City's ears.
They reached a half-inch behind the frames and there sank
into his temples, fusing seamlessly into skin and bone. The
frames for the opaque lenses reached to meld with the skin
over the eye-sockets, preventing Cole from seeing the eyes
behind. If there *were* eyes behind them. There was no

bridgepiece to the shades. Instead, the frame between the lenses was grafted into the skin and cartilage of the bridge of his nose. The mirrorshades were part of his skull.

No one had given the cab driver directions. And he did not speak, not once. He seemed to know where he was going. Cole could barely make out the outline of his head. The meter hadn't been cocked; it registered zero.

Pools of streetlamp light guttered past. The car, a Brazilian *Sabo* fueled by sugarcane alcohol, purred almost soundlessly over the asphalt. The old woman in the front seat was sobbing, and Cole heard her murmur: "Marie . . ."

The cabs pulled up, one behind the other, and everyone climbed out.

They were on Hyde Street, a few blocks from Club Anesthesia, in the Tenderloin district, hooker heaven.

Without waiting for the fare, the cabs rolled away. The man with the thin mustache clutched his robe about him and looked after the cabs in astonishment. His surprise became fear when he realized the cop in the mirror glasses was gone and had left him standing on a street corner at midnight, in his pajamas, surrounded by prostitutes and pimps and Catz and Cole.

Cole tapped him on the shoulder and smiled a smile he hoped was reassuring. Cole felt he should explain. But it would be useless to try to explain that the black man in the backwards baseball cap and mirrorshades talking to the black pimp was the "cop" who'd brought them here, who was not a cop at all but a man who was not a man whom Catz called City. Useless.

So instead: "Your name, sir?" Cole asked brightly.

"Chester Jones, and I want you to know that I'm an attorney and if there is any sort of—"

"Just what in Jesus's Name are we here for?" interrupted the older man in the dark suit.

Cole turned to see City disappear into the old apartment building with the pimp.

Cole was on his own. "I'm, ah, Detective Dubois," Cole improvised. "I—I'm working under cover. What we're doing here—" He hesitated. What *were* they doing there? He blurted, "We're here to reacquaint you with your children."

"My Roy? Have you seen him? Roy Jones? He's—" Mrs. Jones began. "He's a tall, pale sort of kid—"

"My Roy! My Roy!" shrieked the hookers between giggles. A black woman in a blond wig with stardust on her eyelids, did a high five with a white girl wearing a black wig and midnight dust on her eyelids—they took turns mimicking Mrs. Jones's pensive stance, wringing their hands and chanting, "My Royee! My Wit-oo Roy-ee!"

Ignoring the hookers, the lady in the black evening gown asked Cole: "Lucille Schmidt?" She leaned close and implored with her eyes. "You have seen her?"

"Ahh, she'll be taken care of, ma'am," said Cole, not knowing what else to say. He drew Catz aside, "Hey, Catz, psi this for me. You got any idea what he plans to do with 'em? I mean, if their kids are hookers, what good will—"

"He's going to reconcile them with their parents. one way or the other. Either they go with their parents and work things out or they finish their relationship with them another way—they destroy it. Doesn't matter to him, as long as the matter is taken care of, one way or the other. He's testing circuits. No value judgment in it. Hookers are part of a city; he's not particularly opposed to them."

"Hey, did you ever know a hooker to go back home like that—even the young ones—just overnight? Especially with all the others watching. When I was a hustler we—"

"Shit, remember when you were living with those morons on Fifty-third in New York? Weren't there times you felt so down and shitty that if your parents had shown up, right then, maybe for a ten-minute space you were so lonely you would have gone with them . . . right? Wasn't there a time like that?"

"Yeah. Sure. For a few minutes at a time. And if my old man had timed it right . . . I see what you mean. And I guess City would know the ripest time."

Catz pointed at the stairs: There was City, herding a teenager down ahead of him.

"Mom, what the *fuck* are *you* doing here?" asked the girl coming down the steps. She was short, plump and blond; she wore clingpants and a tight sweater, her hair braided, skimpy makeup: She was trying for the college coed look— tricks loved it.

She glared at her father. Her mother ran to her and Lucille surrendered to an embrace, glancing apologetically at the other hookers and rolling her eyes. . . . But two minutes later she refused to let her mother go. She was crying. And violently whispering "Stick it, cunt!" at the laughing streetwalkers. Her father stood by stiffly, about to impose the sternness in his face onto his daughter, when City—once more resembling the plainclothes cop—spoke to Mr. Schmidt: "Your self-righteous attitude is inappropriate. In June, 2002 you paid five thousand dollars to a young man in a blue Chevrolet. Do you remember why you paid that money?"

Schmidt looked into City's face. In the face of all the implacability of the city of San Francisco invested in one man, denials were useless.

Schmidt's face, formerly an unyielding architecture of scowl, a monument to his resentment of his daughter, collapsed into weeping. He threw his arms around his wife and daughter.

Mr. and Mrs. Chester Jones waited, holding hands

beneath a streetlight.

"You're not going to tell me our boy is *here*—" Mr. Jones began.

"That bar," City stated, pointing at the Back Door Club, half a block north. "He's cruising, selling his ass for junk. He's in there now. Go find him. . . ." City put out a hand and touched Jones on the shoulder. Jones shivered and drew his wife close.

"I feel odd," he murmured, rubbing his shoulder. "Like something's *in* me. . . ."

"Roy won't resist you: My authority accompanies you. Just put your arms around him and he will come. He is ripe for surrender. Touch him but say nothing and never judge him."

"I can't go in there like some *street punk,*" Jones objected. "Especially dressed like this. I'm an attorney, I'm the house attorney for Ivory Meats and it's a job with certain responsibilities to the firm's image and—if that's a hangout for streetwalkers, well, I'm not going to mingle with streetwalkers—"

"All of us walk the streets," said City. "Or can you fly? Go on."

Moving slowly, Mr. and Mrs. Chester Jones walked down the street and, holding their bathrobes tight around them, disappeared into the front door of the Back Door Club.

It was one A.M. The traffic was thin, the street was nearly empty, their voices were taking on echoes. Then:

"Marie!" cried the old woman, sitting on the steps. She leapt upright and pushed through the gaggle of marveling hookers. A block down the street a spindly silhouette stopped and stared. "Marie!" called the old woman, running clumsily toward the dim figure.

Marie turned to run the opposite way. Faint through the growl of the city: "Fuck *off* and leave me 'lone!"

She was half a block ahead of her mother and outdistancing her. City nodded his head, almost imperceptibly. The ground briefly trembled. Marie tripped. She fell on her face and lay dazed for thirty seconds, long enough for her mother to catch up.

The pimp loped down the stairs and stabbed a finger at City's chest. "Who the *fuck* you think you be, azzhole? Huh? Where's that brother was here? Dude in the white lid?" When City didn't reply the man adjusted his own dark glasses, mirrorshades looked into mirrorshades and reflected the glassy maskings infinitely. "You *fuckin'* weh me man or *what*? You ain't no fuckin' cop motherfucker. This is *not* part of the deal with SFPD. Hey I'm talking to you motherfucker, I lose that pussy I lose two hundred cold apiece every—" He stopped.

He gaped. He sputtered.

Arm outstretched palm down, fingers spread, City irrigated the asphalt with old-fashioned cash. Hundred-dollarbills were raining from his palm, materializing in thin air between his fingers, spiraling crisp and green to the sidewalk and street. Reflexes took over; no one questioned the phenomenon.

The pimp and the hookers got down on their hands and knees to reap cash. Catz joined them, laughing. Cole picked up a bill and examined it. It was real. He tucked it into his pocket. There was at least ten thousand dollars on the sidewalk when City lowered his arm and gave off raining money. ITF made paper money useless for most transactions, but it could be exchanged for cardcredit at the Interfund main office. One of the hookers, a Chicano with luminous red lipstick and a towering blond wig, decided to cozy to the source of the bounty. She slipped her arms around City and put one hand between his legs. Cole watched her fingers seeking. City didn't move. The woman pressed his crotch. And drew back in horror. "He's—uh— it's like—" she stuttered. "He's all . . ." Covering her mouth with one hand she turned and ran up the steps, vanishing into the building.

Mr. and Mrs. Jones were returning, a gaunt young man between them.

All three were crying. For three different reasons. Mr. Jones was weeping because he was house attorney for a Mafia-owned meat-packing firm which was a front for a pushing ring and his son was a prostitute and though Mr. Jones tried and tried he couldn't recall the important difference in their occupations. And his wife was crying for her son and her son was crying for his dope.

Far down the street, Marie was struggling with her mother. They rolled on the sidewalk, kicking and gouging, both of them in tears. Unthinking, Cole began to walk toward them. The disco music, like an electric mockery of a dirge, accompanied him, getting louder the closer Cole got to them. When he'd almost reached Marie and her mother the song was thundering in his ears and one of the two dark figures on the sidewalk was not moving. The other was lifting one arm high over her head, bringing it down hard on her mother's limp body. "Marie . . ." Cole murmured.

He heard frightened shouting from behind.

The disco music abruptly ceased.

Cole spun and ran toward City and Catz.

Three yellow sedans had formed a U, trapping the front steps of the apartment building where the pimp, the women, and Catz were still stuffing their pockets with money. City stood, legs planted well apart, staring at the headlights.

A cab, as shadowy as the one that had brought Cole, drove past carrying the Joneses, the Schmidts, and their children. The cab passed on the left, turned a corner, was gone.

Catz was getting to her feet, blinking in the headlight glare, as Cole crossed the street onto that block.

A man with shiny gunmetal in his hand was getting out of the nearest yellow sedan.

"Catz, get down!" Cole shouted. "Vigilantes, stupid!"

Six men, nylon stockings flattening their features into pink gargoyles, were pushing the hookers and their man back against the wall. The pimp tried to talk his way out of it, waving handfuls of cash at them; one of the vigilantes kicked him in the stomach; when he doubled up, another vig cracked him across the back of the skull with a gun butt. He sprawled facedown.

One of the hookers shouted, "Hey, you don't impress nobody, asshole!"

The gun fired, red smoke and growling echoes; the hooker's right knee exploded. She fell; her friends bent over her, cursing, crying.

Cole slowed to a walk, thirty feet away, keeping to the shadows. The vigilantes hadn't yet noticed him—they were making too much noise of their own, pawing the shrieking streetwalkers and laughing. Four more vigilantes had gone into the apartment building to flush out the rest of the hookers. They were going to kill them all at once. A police car started to swing onto the street, but seeing the vigs' familiar unlicensed yellow sedans, it backed unobtrusively out; the patrolman could say he'd been distracted by an emergency elsewhere and had seen nothing.

Two of the men in the hose-masks were shouting at City, one of them gave him a warning shove. Or tried to—he held his damaged hand while his friend slapped City across the face with his gun barrel. City stood as if rooted. Once more he wore his trenchcoat and fedora hat. And mirror sunglasses.

The shorter of the two men fired his pistol pointblank at

City's solar plexus. Three times. City jerked slightly but showed no other effect. He stood with his hands straight down at his sides. He opened his mouth. . . .

A siren blasted from his open mouth.

Cole clapped his hands over his ears. The windows beside him rattled violently and the grime caking them shivered off into clouds. It was an alarm siren, yowling from City's throat at fifty times the usual volume. The police would *have* to be attracted. They couldn't pretend an alarm that loud wasn't there.

The vigilantes, hands over ears, piled into their cars.

The sedan pointing toward City backed into the street all the way to the opposite curb, jounced on its shocks, spun its wheels and surged forward. It struck City head-on. The car bucked and bounced back, engine whining. City was standing. But he shook his head as if to clear it. Blood flowed from beneath his pants-cuffs onto his shoes, and from the corner of his open mouth. The ululating siren took on a gurgling undertone but did not falter. The prostitutes took advantage of the vigilantes' distraction. They ran past Cole, down the street and around the corner. Keeping close to the wall, wincing at the siren, Catz sidled up to Cole, eyes on the vigilantes' cars, and Cole pulled her into a dark doorway.

The car backed up again. Its engine coughed and stalled. Another car was already backing down the street, past Cole to the left. He looked around for something to throw, some way to stop it. But it got a full block's acceleration behind it before it struck City. This time he gave way and the car passed over him and piled into the corner where concrete stairway met the brick building's face. . . . It wrenched sideways, its tailfin gouging the brick wall; a shower of concrete dust and a hiss of steam. Then, except for a ticking noise from the car's engine, all was quiet.

All was quiet—for five seconds. Till a police siren sounded, and drew near.

The stalled sedan succeeded in awakening its engine. It plunged after the remaining car which was already half a block down the street and speeding away.

Cole looked at City. City was an oozing heap of cloth and flesh, on the sidewalk twenty feet away. The torn corpse was barely recognizable as human. Cole glanced up at the sky-line of San Francisco, expecting it to buckle and collapse. The city stood as stolidly as ever. So mourning was silly.

Cole looked at the reflecting red-velvet pool of blood hastily stretching its wet fingers to the curb.

The two sedans were just turning the corner.

Cole knew then, seeing the purposeful flowing of City's blood toward the street, that the vigilantes would never make it.

Catz knew it too and she laughed out loud.

The streetlamps that threw themselves in the way of the yellow sedans didn't bend like rubber: They *snapped down*, smashing their lamps on the paving with a strident crash. They clamped the street shut on either side of the sedans. Six of the remaining eight vigilantes jumped free of the cars and ran in panic, swearing and peeling their masks off as they went. Two running south, side by side, were stopped in split-second simultaneity by the metal talons ranking up through the asphalt—at first Cole thought they were immense fingers of black metal. Looking closer, he saw they were four thick utility pipes, slapping downward over the two men like a huge triggered mousetrap. Crushing them instantly. By the time Cole turned to look at the other four, they too were dead. Fat blue sparks still jumped from the broken powerlines binding the spasming corpses.

The ground shivered as directly beneath the single moving yellow sedan two more foot-thick pipes promptly tore up through the asphalt, scattering black street-chunks and blue dust, jamming themselves with a grating squeal up through the oil pan, to either side of the engine block, ramming through the fenders and forcing the engine halfway out of the ruptured hood. Twisted fragments of metal flew, followed by steam and smoke founting from the mangled front end, the car torquing slightly on the impaling shafts, front wheels spinning impotently three feet in the air, the tank exploding, consuming the car in striated red and black.

One of the men had been blown apart, the other had gone through the windshield on impact and was unnaturally embracing the flaming machinery exposed where the hood had been; bent spikes of steel emerged from his back.

Oily black smoke bellied and undulated upward, distorting the faces gawking from windows into demonic leers.

The sirens wailed nearer and were joined by the clangor of fire engines. Cole joined Catz in laughing.

Children ran past to admire the wreck. Cole fell silent, thinking about going home.

"I stay at your place tonight?" Catz asked. They strolled away, with little hurry, threading the crowds pouring from bars and apartment buildings.

"What's it all about f'r Chrissakes?" a Chicano biker asked. Cole shrugged.

"Sure, Catz, you welcome to stay over," Cole said. "I got a couch folds out into a bed."

"Some guy *mashed* over here, man!" someone shouted from behind.

Cole glanced over his shoulder; City's mirror sunglasses gleamed intact from the curb, looking after them.

"Yeah, that'd be great," Catz was saying. "Maybe we could watch TV or something."

Cole pressed through a crowd looking at someone on

the sidewalk, stepped over the body of Marie's mother, and continued on, without looking back.

"Sure," Cole said. "I got Intersat. Ought to be something on." He shrugged. "It's not too late to watch TV."

And they did. They watched some slob who was supposed to be Kennedy in *PT-109*. And afterwards they sat silently by the window and watched the city lights until, at dawn, the lights began to go out; as the cityscape rose grimly into day.

—TEW!

COLE STARED AT THE NOTICE in disbelief. Standing by the window of his flat on a grisly, wet, windy May Monday morning, reading and rereading the notice that had printed out from the public PC. "And it *would* come on a Monday," he muttered. He fingered the imperious red electrostamped letters: PLEASE REMIT SUM OF $3000.00; INTERFUND REGISTRATION. FORWARD TO J. SALMON, BUREAU ELECTRONIC DISBURSEMENT: PAST DUE HANDLING TAXES . . .

"Past due handling taxes." Cole repeated. The coffee-taste in his mouth (his stomach burned, he shouldn't have had coffee on an empty stomach) had gone very sour. *The taste of corruption,* he thought, spitting into the hallway trash can.

Carrying the card, he went into his apartment and closed the door behind him. Moving thoughtfully, he placed the card atop the dusty TV set. He went to the news-box fixed onto the side of the TV, pressed the button, scanned the front page appearing on the screen . . . *PREZ Signs ITF Deadline.* . . . He scanned the page, picking up datashreds . . . *have until November to make the changeover to*

Electronic Exchange Systems. The governors of Louisiana and Washington protested, pleading for more time. . . . Senator Wiley continues to maintain that time enough has been granted, giving the lengthy list of cities already employing Instantaneous Transfer. . . . UN Resolution to petition for funds for Global Village Electronic Exchange Network . . .

And then the news-sheet blinked off. And Cole blinked, astonished. He glanced at the plug. The set was plugged in. Another picture came on, a cartoon, *Fucky Graffiti,* a children's Elementary Pornography program: A sketchy set of male genitalia, independent of a body except that it had its own little legs, chased a runaway vagina. He hit the *off* switch, watched the frantic genitals fade. *What the hell?* He pressed the *on* button again and activated the news-box. "What the fuck's happened to the news?" he mumbled. No news. But—letters in electrostamp style: NEWS-BOX SERVICE CANCELED PENDING PAYMENT BED HANDLING TAX. . . .

"Sonzuvbitches!" he shouted, slapping the set off before *Fucky Graffiti* could make another appearance.

He went to the phone; his fingers automatically ran through the button-pushing, and he watched the small screen impatiently, inwardly fuming, waiting for his lawyer's TV image to flicker on.

"Arthur Topp's office. May I help you?" came a young man's voice. That would be Art's secretary. And lover.

"Yeah . . ." Cole began, staring at the blank comscreen, suspicion mounting. "I need to talk to him. This is Stu Cole."

"Would you prefer to speak without image, sir?" The boy sounded annoyed; it was rude to call without showing yourself, though the party called had the option of keeping screen-blank.

"Uh, no, but—my picture's out. Needs repair or something."

"I see."

A pause, a click. "Stu? Where's your picture? Self-conscious about the way you look on a Monday morning?" Topp's voice. No picture.

"Screen's out—BED turned it off. They turned off my news-box too. They're trying to scare me into paying. They'll turn off the sound on this pretty soon, too."

"Ma BED after you, is she?"

"You think there aren't corporate links between AT&T and ITF? There'd have to be . . ."

"Okay. So, you owe 'em money . . . ?"

"Yeah, I—No! No, they *claim* I owe 'em. That's why I want you."

"You still owe *me* credit." Topp said, more humorously than accusingly.

"Uh-huh. I'll pay it, right away, and half your fee in advance. But listen, it's this handling tax business."

"Oh." There was a note of despair in Topp's voice. "That."

"Look, it's not as if it can't be fought—"

"If you want to take it to the federal courts. But that'll take time. A whole lotta time. The courts are really tied up trying to handle all the suits from that Nuke Terrorist thing in Oregon."

"What? Who are they suing? They never caught the guy so how can they—"

"They're suing the government because supposedly the FBI let him slip through their fingers. Suing 'em for negligence. I mean, the families of a couple hundred thousand people, you know—families spread around the country, relatives. It's stupid of the courts to even consider the suits 'cause they know they'll set a precedent if they award anyone anything and they know the guy—or somebody like him—is gonna do it again. Another city, maybe this one, up in mushroom smoke 'cause some guy with two years college tinkered the thing together and tried to extort—"

"Yeah, well—they'll probably throw it all out. Anyway, we'll have to start somewhere—"

"I mean," Topp interrupted somewhat hastily, "that whole damn town, the whole city of Salem, Oregon, is just *gone,* it's nothing but a crater, and shit, it could happen here."

"You're talking about that stuff because you don't want to talk about the handling tax. Come *on.*"

"Anything you say."

There was silence except for a crackle from the speaker under the small rectangular vidscreen. The screen was mounted over the phone's red plastic touch-tone wedge.

Then Topp said: "Can't do it. You and I know that the handling tax is bullshit, it's the BED boys scraping off the top—"

"Yeah. I don't mind that too much. I'm used to paying protection. But they're springing this back-payment stuff on me *all at once*—I mean, they're giving everyone else a fresh start, man. Years to pay. Me they demand back-payment for all the time I used ITF facilities . . . And do you know *why?*"

"Why?" Topp asked, though he knew. Cole could hear him sucking on a cigarette.

"Because I let the hookers come in my club and they get around all the taxes and the protection stuff, and BED wants to organize 'em. And they don't wanna be organized."

"You're talking dangerous stuff—talking like they're the Mob, f'r Chrissakes." Topp was warning him that the BED buggers were probably listening in.

"Call it what you want." Cole said. "They're after me for that—they warned me—and they know it was me who wrote that petition to let small shops use cash, and they know it was me who—"

"Damn it, Cole!"

"Don't hint I oughta shut up, Topp! They *know*. If they're listening they aren't learning anything new, man."

"Okay. They know it was you who wrote the initiative against the Electronic Switchover." Topp's voice was weary.

Cole hesitated. Something new had occurred to him. "Topp, have they—?"

"Just threats."

"So—you aren't going to take me on?"

"Not unless I want to get tossed out of the Bar Association."

"You can't tell me that's fucking *legal*, man. They can't—"

"Look, the local judges have their own bank accounts and BED can always find an excuse to nail down somebody's credit if they don't play ball. You couldn't get a favorable ruling anywhere in the area. And like I said, the feds are tied up for months. You might go to the, um—" He hesitated; then, reticently, "Well, look . . . uh—"

"Thought better of giving me advice?" Cole asked bitterly.

"I got to go to a lunch. Business lunch, very important."

"Yeah, I'll bet. I hope he bites it off," Cole snarled, stabbing his thumb at the cut-off button.

Cole absently took a cigar from a cabinet beside the phone, lit it, clamped it between his teeth and puffed thoughtfully, sinking his hands in his trouser pockets. He walked to the couch and, staring into space, sat down.

The low red sofa, with its threadbare cushions askew, cut across a corner of the living room. He sat opposite the blank portable TV. The room was entirely off-white, light-panels set flush into the white ceiling. The only decorations were Cole's photographs: pictures of the city. City. Cole was an amateur photographer.

"I'm not going to sell my camera," he murmured, gazing

at the photos. "Not my Nikon. I'll sell the club first." He took a drag on the cigar and said, "Stop talking to yourself, idiot." Then he laughed.

There were more than thirty black-and-white matted photos spaced about the walls, arranged to suggest the demarcations of city blocks. Most of them were highly detailed overview shots taken from the tourist 'copter.

The city like solid-state circuitry.

"I'm not going to sell the club. Fuck those bastards," he said, rather loudly. And he rubbed his balding spot, frowned when he felt a pimple, screwed up his strong, wide mouth. He worried, briefly, about getting old, about his paunch, about his habit of talking to himself, about Pearl and whether he should hire a detective to find her and could he afford a detective anyway. And about the notice from BED. "When?" he asked no one.

He got up, went to the TV, picked up the notice . . . SERVICES PRO CLUB ANESTHESIA TERMINATED APRIL 24 PENDING PAYMENT IN FULL. "April twenty-fourth. They know I can't get that kinda money," he murmured. "And *they* control bank loans." *Stop talking to yourself,* he thought.

"You've been trying hard not to think about me and you're doing it with considerable success," said someone, where there was no one.

"Wha—? Sh-*it!*" Cole exclaimed, his back going rigid, arms crossing his chest with a defensive snap. He looked around. No one there. Until his eyes found the face on the TV screen.

The TV was turned off. But someone was depicted there. Through the screen slid a nictitating line, rippling the image. Then, there he was again. A man's head and shoulders. A talking head.

"City . . ."

"You prefer to forget about me?" the face on the TV

screen inquired. It was in black and white.

"Yeah . . . About what happened. Not about you," said Cole, knees drawn up and clamped together, arms huddling them close. He stared at the stern face on the screen. Mirror sunglasses, rough edges. An unfinished bust in stone. The cold face of the man he'd seen crushed by a car. The city's overmind.

"You'd have a hard time forgetting, once you went out," City said. "You'd hear people talking. If you'd got to the bottom of that news-sheet you'd have seen an article on the police 'investigation' of the deaths of the men killed Saturday night. The ones I killed."

"Shh!" Cole hissed reflectively.

"They're not listening in," City interrupted. "They can't." His lips seemed to move a split second after Cole heard the words said. "I'm part of everything here," City said. "Except BED. That's like a cancer in me." The hard mouth frowned faintly. "I keep them from hearing . . ."

"Look—" Cole relaxed a little, putting his cigar in an ashtray, leaning forward. "If someone else were to come in here while you were speaking to me . . . uh—would they be able to see you?"

"Sure. You're not hallucinating. But don't bother to run and get someone. I'd go off so neither of you could see me. I don't want to talk to anyone but you and Catz."

"All right," said Cole, his voice sounding mechanical in his own ears. "Should I get Catz?"

"No. She's going to hear from me later. . . . Just now, I've got something to show you." The TV picture changed. Now it was a black-and-white shot—from ceiling level, a corner—of four men sitting around a table in a plush office beside a plate glass window. "Do you recognize the man at the head of the table, Cole?" City's image was gone, but his voice came to Cole clearly, with all the hearty friendliness of the Time Operator counting off the minutes over a phone.

Cole looked at the man at the head of the table. A broad, florid man with thick glasses and white hair (probably a hair piece) and long white sideburns. "Rufe Roscoe. The mobster."

"Yes. The others?"

The guy with the carrot-fuzz for hair and the freckles and the stupid leer was—

"Salmon. The Interfund attorney."

"Yes. You don't know the rest?"

"No."

"Then listen . . ."

Other voices came from the TV's speaker grid. Salmon was saying, ". . . Rusk sold us his share for what he paid for it because of the tax issue! Boswell made a profit, four percent; that gave us forty-two percent, so we went to—"

"Never mind," said Roscoe impatiently, "What do we have *now?*"

Salmon smiled. "Fifty-three percent."

"Beautiful!" said Roscoe, though his face reflected no awe for beauty. He looked as if he'd just killed something, and enjoyed it.

"But . . ." Salmon began hesitantly.

Roscoe leaned forward.

Salmon said: ". . . there's this fellow Topp, and he and the DA are talking about indictment, illegal stock acquisition, maybe a freeze on collecting—"

"The DA," Roscoe interrupted. His interruption was spoken softly, but Salmon, attentive, quieted instantly. Roscoe leaned back. "The DA is an old man. If he had a heart attack no one would be surprised. There's a doctor I know . . . Well, just take the guy out of the picture. And maybe Topp too."

"It would be better just to scare Topp. If too many in that connection start to disappear—"

"All right. If he knows we control the majority shares of ITF he'll come home wagging his dick behind him. . . ." Roscoe smirked, glancing absently out the window.

The image fell into darkness; was replaced by City.

"Where'd you get that?" Cole asked.

"Roscoe's an eccentric about recording everything, like Nixon and the White House tapes, only he didn't learn from Nixon's mistake. But he does it because the syndicate boys only rat on each other when they can cover their own naked pink tails, and he figures he keeps irrefutable audiovisual records of his dealings with his boys, if they ever try to testify against him from cover, with FBI protection, he'd be able to take them down with him. With this stuff, somebody would have to prosecute them. It's something the board members know about, and it's a deterrent against betrayal. He sets up the camera himself, unloads it himself. He keeps the films in a vault."

"Stupid of him. The risk that the cops'll get hold of 'em without his go-ahead is more dangerous than what he wants to prevent. Keeping the tapes is just dumb. If the feds got a court order to open that vault . . ."

"Yes," said City, "Fortunately he doesn't realize that. He's a fanatic about his own notions and pretty stubborn. Thinks he's infallible."

"So why don't you show this to the police commissioner, on *his* TV?"

"He's in BED's bed. Besides, I couldn't communicate with him. Not easily. He'd think he was going mad. You— it's as if you invoke me, in a way. I can get through to you. Anyway, as sole evidence the tapes wouldn't work, since *our* access to them is illegal. Evidence illegally acquired."

"I see. Because we'd have to steal it. And at this point it

would be hard to convince the feds to get a court order. . . . Hey—how did you show me tapes he keeps in a vault?"

"That one is in his editing machine. He was looking it over, just now, watching the faces of his associates, looking for duplicity, and he was interrupted. He left the editor set up in the vault. I ran it back and ran it through again, transmitting it here through the electrical connection. Its power source—"

"But this is a TV!"

"No, it's a part of *me*. A TV is a media outlet for the city. A neuron in my brain. The means I use to transfer the image from video to electron-patterns, bring it through the wires and feed it into your TV—it's a form of telekinesis. Manipulating electronics with thought. At night I have the power in every cerebral battery in the city. A brain stores electricity. I can tap in, when they sleep. . . . During the day I have only the power of those who sleep in the day—far fewer, so I'm limited. Though I'm bolstered by people watching TV, since that's a form of sleeping, . . . I'm the sum total of the unconscious cognition of every brain in the city. And I'm Rufe Roscoe, too—I'm his self-hatred."

He paused while Cole tried to take it all in.

Then City asked: "Why do you think I picked *you*, Cole?"

"Why?"

"Because . . . You're not screaming in panic now. You're nervous, but you're not disoriented. Most people would be terrified if I appeared to them like this, talking to them directly, telling them these things. You instinctively understand the Greater Urban Reality. The secret geometries of the city."

"Huh . . . If you say so."

"Besides, Cole, you've got portraits of me, all over your walls."

Cole smiled.

City didn't.

"So," Cole began, looking away, "I suppose you—you're gonna want me to do—*do* something for you. Right?"

"They have to be stopped."

"The Mob?" Cole glanced at the remittance notice and nodded. "My club is all I've got to live for."

"Yes. The Mob. . . ."

Just the Mob? Cole wondered.

"Maybe," Cole began, "I could hire someone to break into the vault, steal the tapes, use them as evidence for the newspapers, if not the feds—"

City shook his head. "No, they couldn't get in without my help. *You* might—but they'd kill you, once you had them. First, we'll encourage divisiveness in their organization. Set them at one another's throats; and we'll save the videotapes till they're weak and bring them out when we have BED in court. We'll give them to the papers then, turn the juries against them. I can get you to them, eventually. But there are other things you must do first. It has to be you."

Cole shook his head.

City nodded grimly.

Cole shook his head violently. "Hey—I can help you plan, I can find people to—to do the work for you. But I'm not competent to do it myself. I'm not James Bond, pal. I'm in bad shape."

"You're the only one I can work with. You and that woman. And perhaps not even her. We'll see about her."

"What the hell can *I* do?"

"A great deal, with my assistance. You saw what happened to the vigilantes. So-called."

Cole considered. He retrieved his cigar from the ashtray and relit it, puffing purple clouds. "They're going to take away my club," he said, to convince himself. "There's nothing else for me. So I get killed, so what?" But his hand shook and ashes fell prematurely from his cigar's ember.

"I thought I had it made ten years ago, when I bought the club. Thought it'd be easy. Every week it's been a struggle just to—"

"Cole," City interrupted, "I can help you stop them. I can make things happen that will be useful. But *only at night*. Remember that. I can *speak* to you in the day . . . at times."

"I understand."

"Bring the woman here tonight, at seven."

"Catz? She might have a gig—"

"She'll come. I can speak to you through technology— but I have a stronger psychic link with her. She's a *sensitive*. She'll be useful, for a while anyway."

"What do you mean, *for a while?*"

City ignored the question. "Have your assistant run your club tonight. You and Catz will buy masks and guns. You'll go to the Pyramid Building. You'll go to the eighteenth floor. There will be guards. We'll take care of them."

Fear caught in Cole's throat. The giddiness was gone. His heart was leaden—and, on his mental screen, he seemed to see himself with a marksman's target pinned to his chest. Cole cleared his throat, managed:

"Look—I don't feel prepared to kill anyone. Not just yet. I can't just now."

"You won't have to—just yet." City said, his voice becoming harsh. The TV image flickered, vanished . . . and reappeared, a little fuzzier. "I can't stay in contact much longer, Cole. So listen—I'll be there with you tonight. I can't manifest again in physical form, not unless I find the perfect vessel, someone right for the possession . . ."

Something as cold and as burning as dry-ice made Cole shiver from the spine. *The perfect vessel . . .*

City (his voice becoming progressively less audible) went on: "I have to go—I'll be there with you tonight. She'll feel me there, and you'll know. But I can't kill them, not yet. They're part of the syndicate—they'd only be replaced by others. We've got to get it out of the city—BED itself is—"

"I don't know," Cole muttered. "I'm not sure that's desirable even if it's possible—"

All this time City's voice had been even. But now it was ragged with rage, and accompanying it was a high-pitched whistle, a painful shrilling that made Cole wince. "*It* is a puppetmaster for us all, Cole. ITF is disease masked as convenience! Bring the woman here tonight."

And then the screen went blank.

Cole sat staring at the blank screen. All he could think about was a disturbing quality in City's voice. As City had denounced ITF as a puppetmaster part of some vast conspiracy, Cole had been reminded of another voice he'd heard—another time. A voice over the telephone when once for a joke he and Catz had called the American Nazi party's hotline, and listened, snickering, to ravings about the Jewish Communist-Negro Homosexual Conspiracy. The Nazi's voice had a tone of unassailable unreasonableness. . . . City's tone.

But somehow Cole knew he would do as City had asked.

Cole looked at the photos on the walls. He could never leave the city.

"If he's going to help us, why do we need the guns?" Catz asked.

They sat together in the front seat of a rented car. In the darkness. Between them, on the curving vinyl seat, was a paper sack, its top crimped and neatly folded. It contained two .38s and two rubber masks.

"You stood there and listened too," Cole said, glancing at his watch. At the briefing—so brief it validated the term—they hadn't had time to ask City questions. He'd rattled off instructions from the TV.

"He didn't really explain that, though. About the guns."

"It's because there are armed guards and the men in the board room may be armed. Roscoe will be, at least. And City can't do everything for us. So we have to use the guns to bluff them—"

"Wave them in their faces? That's all?"

"Let's hope so."

Cole's hands were clammy on the fiberglass of the steering wheel, and his palms made sucking noises when he pulled them away to wipe cold sweat on his trousers.

"We're not questioning him," she remarked. There was no alarm in the observation.

Cole nodded. "It's weird. But—that's probably why he picked us—we are, uh—we're like—" Cole struggled for words.

"Metropolitan aborigines. Wilderness aborigines aren't suspicious when they get the word from nature spirits."

"Maybe that's it," Cole conceded, realizing that they were discussing abstractions only to take their minds off the risk they were about to take. He glanced at his watch. His heart quailed. "It's time," he said.

Catz reached into the back seat, dragged into the front a large imitation-leather totebag containing a cassette tape recorder. "I hope it's true about voiceprints being special from person to person. Or all this"—she stuffed the masks into the totebag, put her arm through the strap-loop—"may be for nothing."

Moving fatalistically, Cole thrust the loaded revolver in the inner pocket of his coat, so that it rested butt upwards against his left pectoral. He covered the bulge with an overcoat draped over his left shoulder. Catz put her own pistol in the handbag. And they got out of the car. Both wore army surplus fatigues over regular clothes.

The car doors' slamming seemed loud, and Cole jumped at the sound. Steadying himself, he walked through the mild May evening to the front of the elongated Pyramid Building. "Eighteenth floor," he muttered to himself.

The street was deserted: This was a business district, and after hours it was nearly dead. Streetlife called faintly from Market Street, a few blocks away. A single car cruised the street, seemed to slow as it drew near Cole, and he had to make an effort to keep from running. But the car cruised on, turned a corner, was gone.

And then they were at the entrance to the building. Pausing, Cole looked up.

The pyramid-shaped building, long and narrow, was nearly lifeless, except for three windows glowing from the eighteenth story.

Cole looked at Catz, swallowing. Catz tugged at his arm. Together they pushed through the glass doors.

An armed Burns Security Guard stood beside the elevator. But he had his back to them. Cole followed the direction of the guard's stare: The man was gaping at two extinguishers on the wall of the corridor leading off to the right of the elevator; the fire extinguishers were spraying foam wildly, their hoses jouncing with pressure, the chrome metal cylinders vibrating against the wall with a monotonous clangor. The guard—staring at the manic extinguishers, not seeing Cole and Catz—walked down the hall, shaking his head, wondering what to do. Trying to avoid the shooting foam, he reached gingerly for the nozzles, seeking a switch that would cut off the flow. . . .

Cole and Catz, hands on the butts of their pistols, went

to the elevator. The doors immediately opened for them. They glanced at the guard, but his back was still to them. They stepped into the elevator, and Cole fancied he could hear Catz's heart pounding in time with his own. They exhaled simultaneously as the doors closed behind them. They didn't have to press the button—the tab of FLOOR 18 lit up and the elevator began to ascend.

"Thank you, City," Cole breathed, expecting no response.

But from the intercom beside the floor-selection tabs came City's voice: "Put on your masks. Others are upstairs. Two more legitimate guards and two hired guns, in the hall and inner office respectively. The Burns guards upstairs know that someone has entered the building without authorization—they keep an eye on the elevator floor indicator and the downstairs guard is supposed to call up when someone enters—so they'll likely have drawn their guns. I'll distract them, but be prepared to use your guns—try to disarm them quietly."

They drew out their rubber masks—sad hobo faces, alike—and put them on. Immediately, Cole's skin began to sweat, to itch in contact with the rubber.

It was close and sticky inside the unreal face.

Cole drew his gun, and the elevator doors opened.

thuh-*REE!*

THERE WAS A DEAD MAN, bleeding on the rug. And over him, there was another man holding a smoking gun. Both men wore uniforms; the man standing was weeping. "Hey—it's not like it looks, man!" he said, turning to the elevator. "The gun went off . . ." Then he saw their masks.

He raised his gun and fired.

Cole and Catz had already flattened themselves against the side walls of the elevator. Cole was frozen with indecision: Shoot back? Close the elevator doors? Surrender?

But Catz fired once and the guard toppled with a bullet in his gut. He writhed on the rug at their feet, calling someone's name.

Oh Christ, Cole thought. *On TV they die right away.*

The man lay on his stomach, squalling like a slapped infant, trying to staunch the bloodflow at his shattered belly with his hands, his face white, his cap wobbling beside him where it had fallen as if it were rocking in sympathy.

Cole raised his gun and, whimpering a little, fired at the man's head. Again. Again. Two of the bullets missed. One struck the man in the rear of his right shoulder.

Slapping Cole's gun down, Catz asked, "What are you *doing?*"

"Trying to—to put him out of . . ." Cole began haltingly.

"I didn't mean to hit him there: I was aiming for his legs. He might live through it. Give him the chance."

"You think, uh, City, ah—made his gun go off to kill the other?"

Catz had no time to reply. They were attacked from two directions. From the front, two balding lumpy men in dark suits came at them with drawn .45s, emerging from the reception vestibule outside the conference room. Already the guards were squeezing their triggers, and— their guns didn't go off. They looked down at them in astonishment, while from the right, trundling down the hall, was an autosecur, one of the simple-minded robots first put on the market in 1979 as guards for warehouses and closed department stores. "Freeze where you are and do not move under any circumstances," came a commanding maternal voice from the robot's globular chromium head. Its arms, continuously jointed like a vacuum cleaner's hose and ending in blunt clamps, swung up and encircled both of the startled gunmen. It repeated its "Freeze where you are . . ." litany which muffled the taller man's protest, "Hey whadduhfuck you doing, bozo, you supposed tuh—" He was interrupted when his buddy's efforts at breaking free triggered a brilliant strobe-flash from the autosecur's head which, at that range, temporarily blinded both guards.

Cole and Catz blinked away colored whorls of distortion in the strobe's afterimage.

The men in the autosecur's arms continued to flail, swearing and shaking their heads as if that would clear away the blindness. A small red light flashed on and off on the robot's cylindrical chest, and at the same time the gunmen jerked and shuddered as the computer pumped short electrical shocks into them. Then they slumped, exhausted and confused; one of them began to weep; gas hissed from a vent at the juncture of the machine's head and chest, and—giggling like hysterical children from inhalation of nitrous oxide—the guards allowed themselves to be towed away, down the hall. . . .

Across the hall, through the open door of the vestibule, Cole could see the door to the conference room opening. "Hey what the hell's the deal?" someone as yet unseen demanded as the door swung outward. "We're trying to—"

Cole wanted to turn and run but Catz, whom he suspected was enjoying the whole affair, sprang forward, gun upraised, tugging her hobo-mask lower on her head with the other hand. "Get the hell back in there!" she shouted, in a contrived gravelly voice.

Cole ran after her, the room dancing about the sweat-sticky eyeholes of his mask. His nose was full of the smell of rubber.

The man framed in the doorway, amazed expression framed by his jowls, backed up convulsively and fell over onto his wide rump. Catz and Cole pressed into the room, waving their guns.

Someone shouted, "Shit, it's a kidnapping!"

There were five men, counting the terrified lump on the floor, and Cole recognized only Rufe Roscoe and his attorney, Salmon.

Two of the men looked not at all frightened: Roscoe, and an out-of-towner (judging from his New York-cut suit), a sallow-faced man with dark circles under his eyes and a polite businesslike smile on his fishy lips.

Cole remembered his lines: "Okay," he said to Salmon, hoping he sounded ruthless, "which ones you want me to kill? All of 'em or just *the one* we talked about?"

The out-of-towner turned a mild but inquiring glance at Salmon. And, seeing the man's profile, Cole recognized him. Gullardo, the Mafia messageman. Cole'd seen Gullardo's picture in profile, in a magazine article. Beneath his mask, Cole smiled: The boys from the national syndicate would be touchy about a hit at a meeting attended by one of their own. Fine.

Cole raised his gun and pointed it at Gullardo. "You want me to kill him or not?" he asked Salmon.

"Wha—uh—*no!*"

"You changed your mind?" Cole asked. And that's when the gun went off.

He stared down at the gun in amazement.

He hadn't pulled the trigger. But Gullardo collapsed, choking on blood, his throat torn open.

"Oh *shit,* City!" Cole said, backing off.

He turned and ran. Catz followed him, shouting something he couldn't make out. A hole appeared in the door-jamb to his right as he passed through, and splinters stung his cheek.

The elevator doors were open, waiting. Catz and Cole dodged into the elevator and flattened against the side walls. Another bullet bit the wall near the ceiling, a few inches from Cole's head. *"Oh-Christ-oh-shit-oh-damn,"* The elevator doors closed. Something dented them slightly from the other side with a metallic *spang*. And then the inner doors closed and they were descending. Seventeenth floor . . . twelfth . . . eighth . . . fifth . . .

"Stop at the second floor, City!" Cole yelled. "Let us out there and we'll take the stairs, otherwise the guards'll be waiting for us at the first—"

But the elevator passed the second floor and opened onto the first. Catz and Cole ducked, Catz fired wildly through the opening. At no one. The bullet penetrated the plate glass windows, leaving a corona of intricate crack-webbing around its puncture.

The guard wasn't in sight. Cole followed Catz, cautiously, out of the elevator. To the left, twenty feet down the hall, the first guard they'd seen lay on his stomach. There was a fire extinguisher next to him. The hose ran over the rug to his face and the nozzle—

"Through the eye!" Cole hissed in disgust.

Impulsively, Cole ran down the hall trying office doors till he found one, three doors down, unlocked. Inside on the receptionist's desk, a telephone. He punched 0 for Operator, remembered to shut off his image so they couldn't screen who was calling. "What are you doing?" Catz asked. "We've gotta get the fuck *outta* here!"

"Calling an ambulance . . ." Cole said.

The operator didn't answer. Instead, City's voice: "Get away fast, Cole. I can only stop their calls to their associates for a short time more—"

"There are people *mangled* here," Cole said, his voice high and thin, "and they need—"

"They need to die," said City's voice, a voice cold and echoey as a downtown street on a winter midnight. "The fewer witnesses the better. BED will cover over the whole incident so their connection with Gullardo is not brought out in the investigation. They'll move him, claim he was murdered elsewhere—"

Cole, taut with rage, slammed his hand on the button that cut the connection. Catz waited for him, fidgeting in the hall.

Moving stiffly, he followed Catz out to the car. . . .

They removed the masks and the fatigues a few blocks south, and Cole wiped sweat from his face. "I think I'm going to break out in hives from that rubber," he muttered.

Catz drove in silence.

Cole asked (because he needed to hear her speak), "You think the cops'll come?"

"No. City would block the call to them. I don't think they'll want the cops in on this till they get rid of Gullardo. If he's dead."

"That—" Cole's stomach was twisting. He swallowed bile. "That's what City said . . . on the phone . . . Wouldn't let me call an ambulance."

There was something between them, in the air, that frightened them both; it was an unspoken realization: City had lied to them.

"Things didn't turn out . . . like he said. . . ." Cole finally murmured.

Defensively, though she wasn't defending herself, Catz said, "Hey Stu—cut him some slack. He can't control *everything*. He isn't Zeitgeist itself. He has to improvise too as things come up." Somehow it seemed, then, that she was defending City only to spare Cole's feelings; to keep him from panicking.

"I didn't pull the trigger on Gullardo," Cole said in a dead voice. "City didn't have to—"

"What?" She looked suddenly at him, almost forgetting about driving. Cole instinctively stabbed his foot at a nonexistent brake when they nearly ran a red light. Half into the intersection, she stopped and pulled back. The street here was nearly empty, except for a few shadowy figures seen through the smoked glass window of a dimly-lit bar, down the steep hill to the right.

"I didn't shoot him. I didn't pull the trigger. City made the gun go off."

"Well maybe—" She cut it short as the light turned green and she had to press the accelerator; the car went backwards. "City, stop it!"

She hit the brake and the car jerked to a stop.

"You had it in reverse," Cole said, smiling a little. "When you overshot the intersection and had to back up, you—"

"Oh!" she smiled sheepishly and put the car in drive, relaxed as it slid ahead. "Oh yeah." She hesitated. "Anyway—maybe City didn't know Gullardo was going to be there and killing him was the only way in that circumstance. But—man, I don't know why it'd have to be necessary. . . ."

Cole realized he was sitting bolt upright, his back rigid and trembling. He made a conscious effort to relax and his body shook a little. He slumped against the door and pressed the tab that rolled the window down; he inhaled cool fresh air. "I need a drink."

"Or maybe . . ." she continued, worrying her lower lip with her incisors, "Maybe you *did* pull the trigger. You can't be sure it wasn't, like, an accident. Your finger sort of jumping . . ."

Cole's forehead furrowed. Perhaps he had; perhaps City hadn't.

Hadn't *what?* he thought savagely. "Killed," he murmured aloud, to get used to the sound of it.

"You'd *better* get used to it," Catz said.

"I don't like it when you read my mind when I don't ask you to," he said softly.

"Sorry. I just picked up a flash, accidentally."

"Yeah. Right. Sure. Bullshit."

"Look, don't get pissed off at *me*, Stu. It's not me you're mad at."

"How you know what the fuck I'm mad at?" His voice quavered. He stared straight ahead. "Unless you're reading my mind."

"I'm not. I can't do it all the time, anyway. I know what you're mad at because I know *you*. And I can see it in the way you're holding your hands like that. Like you're trying to keep from pounding your own face with your fists, slutter. Cred it: you got a personal debt to pay. Just don't slide it onto me. I ain't co-signing for your guilt."

Cole was shaking. He tried to stop. and he couldn't. He felt he was going to shake and shake till the car started to rattle apart with it. He felt taut, suffocated. "Let me out here," he said suddenly. "I need to stretch. I'll see you at the club. I gotta think."

She stopped the car abruptly. *"Maybe* I'll see you at the club."

He climbed out. She threw the car into gear before he had a chance to close the door; the car leaped away, its sudden lurch slamming the door shut, as if the car were itself angry.

He looked around, realizing he had no idea where he was.

He was on Polk Street. He took a deep breath and shivered. The night seemed colder than it should have been.

A tall, flaxen-haired woman dressed as conventionally as a receptionist lectured to a group of four teenage hustlers. "I don't *care* if you don't believe it—you're going to find out about it. Cred *that.* The union is the only thing that's going to protect you from the vigs in the long run, and from the cops and the other creeps that try to fuck you over." She was the Prostitute Union's rep.

Cole drifted out of earshot. He walked past a tavern, through the blast of warm air from its out-vent; it exhaled the scents of beer and wine and 'loid smoke and tobacco, the sounds of contentious drunks trying to be heard over one another.

He passed a late-night video/CD-ROM store, strolling through its pool of colored lights, the roar of its music. He was traveling through a neighborhood that was almost en-

tirely homosexual. It was a cheerful neighborhood, overflowing with laughter and affection. The gays accepted
everyone, for the most part, and sometimes he went to gay
bars to watch men flirt with men and women flirt with
women, to watch men caress men and . . . He enjoyed the
sense of communality in their caresses, the general loose-
ness, their joyful rebellion. More than once Cole had
regretted his heterosexuality. Sometimes he thought wist-
fully he might rediscover his own sexual fire if he could
love communally as the gays did, now that they had the
vaccine.

He passed a gaggle of drag queens; he listened distantly
to their conversation. . . . "Well Miss *Thing*, jus' loookit you,
honey, you gone crazy with that hair color. Nobody wears
green now'days honey, cars gonna mistake you for a traffic
light and run right ovuh you."

Cole smiled vaguely. It wasn't working. He was trying to
lose himself in the city. And it wasn't working. He was insulated by his own pain.

And he was walking too fast. The bearded men in army
boots and jeans, gay motorcycle knights in leather with the
seat of their pants cut away, couples and triples and crowds
of eight and ten passing joints and kissing and making
meaningless jokes, on the sidewalks ahead of him—he kept
having to press through them. A drag queen glared at him
and said, "Well, don't walk on my *heels,* girl, I just bought
those bitches."

"Sorry," Cole mumbled, pushing desperately on.

His heart was pounding.

He was trying to outrun the image . . . trying to repress
it . . . glimpsing:

*There was a dead man, bleeding on the rug. And over him,
there was another man holding a smoking gun.*

Cole turned in at the nearest bar, pushed rudely

through the throng at the counter, and shouted, "A straight bourbon!" at the bartender. The bartender, a little, wizened auntie who'd dyed his hair too many times, pursed his lips and clicked his tongue at Cole.

The jukebox played a very old Pet Shop Boys tune. . . . The bartender looked into Cole's eyes and understanding dawned on him. He shrugged and poured Cole's drink. He poured a double. Cole took the drink to an empty corner booth and sat, sipping, shuddering with the stiff drink, trembling at the effort of repressing. . . .

And failing.

The man lay on his stomach, squalling like a slapped infant, trying to staunch the flow at his shattered belly with his hands . . .

"City . . ." Cole said hoarsely, to nothing, no one.

Cole raised his gun and, whimpering a little, fired at the man's head. Again. Again. Two of the bullets missed. One struck the man in the rear of his right shoulder . . .

"City!" Cole said, between clamped teeth, his eyes screwed shut.

. . . Gullardo collapsed, choking on blood, his throat torn open . . .

"CITY!" Cole shouted, his eyes snapping open.

"You okay, hon?" A little man with a neat goatee and an earring. He smiled faintly. Someone else came to the table . . . a drag queen, Cole noted dully. He downed his drink in three gulps, wincing, and stood.

"Girl, you're looking *awful,"* the drag queen said as Cole sidled past, "—you'd better go home an'—"

"Yeah," Cole said. "Yeah, thanks. That's what I'm gonna do. Go home." He went, blinking, out the door.

Cole passed blindly down the street, murmuring apologies, breathing heavily, dimly aware that he was moving by gay discos, gay movie theaters, gay policemen holding hands as they patrolled their beat, gay holovid specialty stores. He marched furiously to anywhere.

At last he stopped and shook himself. He took a deep breath, and got his bearings. He felt calmer now. He was downtown, near Embarcadero Center; gasohol cars purred to his right, skyscrapers stood hard and cold and sharp-edged in the streetlighting overhead. The sidewalks were almost empty. On his left, someone slumped in a darkened doorway.

Cole stiffened. The dark figure squatting in the door-way's shadow wore mirror sunglasses, a battered hat, and a long coat. Muted music came softly from its mid-section. . . .

"City?" Cole whispered, moving nearer. He bent over the sleeping shape. *"City?"* The man in the doorway reeked of vomit and wine. Cole's eyes adjusted to the darkness. He stared at the man's face; the dark glasses were askew, loose on the nose. The man was asleep, snor-ing softly, hawkish Chicano face coarse with acne. The music came from a small portable radio, half-hidden in the crook of his arm. It was a rock station, phasing in and out, crackling with static.

Cole turned away, sharply disappointed.

"How do you feel, Cole?"

City's voice, from behind.

Cole turned back to the dark figure sleeping, knees drawn up, in the doorway. The man was still snoring.

"City?"

"Yes, Cole." The voice came from the radio, over-riding the music.

Cole moved closer, and bent near the radio, speaking softly so as not to wake the sleeping drunk. "City . . . I'm fucked up. I'm hurting."

"How? Why, Cole?" the radio asked. And then the music resurged as it waited for his answer.

"I'm disgusted. I'm sick with disgust. It's funny . . . at first I didn't feel too bad. In shock or something, I guess. And then I started, um, shaking and it hit me. I killed that man. You and I both killed him. You lied to me about that. And that guard. Maybe Gullardo had to die, maybe he deserved getting his—shit!—his throat shot open. . . . But that security guard, he didn't know anything about it."

"He was stoned, Cole. That guard was stoned and paranoid. He was going to shoot whoever came out of that elevator."

"Even if that's true, there should have been some other way to deal with him than to—"

"There should have been, but there wasn't." City's voice came more loudly, strident. The drunk twitched and whimpered in his sleep.

"Look, I can't do that stuff, I can't—I can't take responsibility for it. I can't pass judgment on these people and blow them away. I don't like the way it looks or the way it feels. . . ." Cole stopped to clear his throat. He was sobbing. The cars moaned behind him. He looked to both sides on the sidewalk. No one coming.

"This had to happen, Cole. This moment of recognition in you. It starts out with hurt and fear and disorientation, and then you recognize yourself, and your role, and you understand."

"No man. I don't understand at all."

"Cole—you didn't shoot those men. *I* did. Maybe I used you to do it. You were the vehicle for me. But really, it was my choice and my responsibility—"

"But I have a choice—or I *should*—as to whether or not I'm going to be your fucking *vehicle.*"

"Uh-uh. No, Stu, that choice was made a long time ago. You were chosen—but at the same time you volunteered. You agreed to be a part of me, to be my agent, long before you ever saw me in your club. And here's something very important, Stu: What *am I?* What do you think I am?"

Cole hesitated. "You're—the unconscious of the city. Collectively. Pooled together somehow. That's what Catz says."

"That's fairly close. But think—what are the implications of that? I'm fulfilling the frustrated desires of all the people in this city. They're secretly afraid of ITF and BED and the computerization of the world and the decentralization of the city. They're afraid of the men who are using those things to gradually take control of them. In spite of the conditioning that makes them want to consciously accept it, *un*consciously they want to fight back. And they've created me so they can do that, and chosen you to be my hands. It was *they,* Stu, who shot Gullardo. It was they who killed the vigs on the street. And you have always been in favor of letting the majority rule, letting people express themselves collectively. You've always been on their side. You are simply carrying out their commands. You are their child. They are your family."

Cole thought about it. It worked. It clicked, for him. It was a functional rationale. It didn't matter whether or not City was morally right. What mattered was: Cole had a justification for the things he'd done that night. The blood was no longer on his hands alone. He shared the guilt with everyone around him. Who was there to judge him? He felt lighter. He shuddered, but this time with relief.

"Okay," he said.

"There will be times," City went on, "that you will doubt them, and me, and you will want out. Maybe even later tonight. But you know how to deal with it now. It will pass. Don't let *anyone* play on your sense of moral guilt, Cole."

Whom did City mean? Catz?

The radio crackled, and mewed inane music once more.

City's voice was gone.

But his presence was there, now, strong in the cluster of buildings around Cole.

Cole walked on, smiling with relief. He felt loose. The tension was gone from him. He thought about his club and turned the corner, heading in that direction: to Anesthesia.

It came to him that he had turned toward his Club as a man's thoughts turn toward the full realization of an idea, or the reliving of a memory. The city was like a great mind, a matrix of ideas, concepts pressed into concrete and asphalt, and he was the center of consciousness traveling that mind, touching on first one idea—one location in the city—and then another, the street addresses laid out in orderly array, one leading to the next, like the pathways of free association.

He felt, more than ever, a part of City's mind.

"Hey, Stu!" He looked up, and saw Catz standing in front of the Club Anesthesia. He smiled and waved. She seemed relieved. She came and took his hand and they walked into the clamor of the nightclub together. By silent mutual agreement they talked of anything, everything—except City, and the dead men in the Pyramid.

They went into the back room, and Cole poured them each a beer. They talked about music, and the audience, and almost managed to forget.

But there was just a little accusation in Catz's tone. She was fighting with herself, to keep from talking about it. Cole felt the self-disgust begin to return. *It's not in my hands,* he told himself. *Everyone in the city decided for me.*

He stood, and stretched, and said he'd better do some work. Catz nodded, looking at the floor. Cole went into the barroom.

For two hours he lost himself in work. He mixed drinks

and fed the multimouthed monster; he washed glasses and worked the till and wiped down the bar; he adjusted the compudisco and examined ID cards and ousted rowdies and pretended to listen to anecdotes he couldn't hear over the din; he poured more drinks and more.

Sometimes he did all these things one after another, with tasks overlapping, in five minutes time, the best speed-bar style; whizzing back and forth behind the bar like a pool ball rebounding from the sides of a pocket. It was a great comfort. He could be a functional part of the machinery of the city night, and he felt at home.

He poured drinks, lubricating the cogs of the Saturday Night Blowoff Machine, and kept a watchful eye over his smoky-dim mirrorball-spangled domain.

The buzzing of Interfund units, the clatter of the dishwasher, the jungle sounds of milling patrons—all merged into one sea-crashing of sound.

He was captain of the Club Anesthesia. He was the Head Doctor administering forgetfulness in shotglass syringes, and he could very nearly forget about writhing security guards and the Italian with the ripped throat on the eighteenth floor of a building designed to survive earthquakes . . . Could forget for a half-hour at a time. And then he'd remind himself that *the whole city pulled the trigger; I just executed their command.*

But now and then he saw the pyramidal building alter to resemble the pyramid on the old printed dollar bills: topped with a great, glowering eye.

They'll be looking for me, he thought, *when they figure out that Salmon didn't set them up. I'm a prime suspect: They know I've got reason to hate them.*

So he was not surprised when, at ten o'clock, after Catz's band had played for an hour, two grey-suited men came in and moved purposefully toward the bar. The older one wore yellow-tinted glasses and his narrow face was further thinned by burn scars pinching the cheeks. The other was a shorter young man, dark, with brown eyes and jet hair; probably a Chicano.

The scarred man said, "Cole? Drummond," and indicated himself with an almost imperceptibly cocked thumb. He nodded sideways at his companion. "Officer Hulera." Drummond showed a wallet-badge.

His faint smile remaining despite the movement of his lips, Hulera asked, "You were expecting us? Someone give you the word?"

"What? Uh—" *Don't stutter,* Cole told himself. "No, shit no. But I know a couple of cops when I see them. You're not the regular patrol come in here to look busy."

Drummond seemed satisfied with that. But Hulera asked, "No idea what we want to talk to you about?"

"Oh quit playing games with him," Drummond said to Hulera irritably. "The guy's not dumb. . . . Cole, you hear anything about some boys at the Crocker Bank building getting hurt?"

"Boys?" Cole asked, trying to sound bored. "You mean kids?"

"I mean guards. One of them was hurt in an awfully unpleasant way."

"Awfully nasty, all right," Hulera put in, shaking his head, his smile gone. "Got an extinguisher hose through the eye."

"Uh—silly way to die." Cole swallowed to stop gagging. "How the hell that happen?" He asked with what must have been a sickly grin.

"We were going to ask *you* that," said Hulera.

"So why me?"

"We've been told you owe a lot of money to those people. A *lot*. The ones on the eighteenth floor of that building," Drummond said, "And you were real pissed off about it."

Cole could feel Drummond's scrutiny. The man was examining minutely every flicker in Cole's expression.

"Hey Drummond," Cole replied. *"Sure* it'd get me out of debt to go to their office and stick things in the eyes of their guards. Oh right. I mean, some fucking *maniac* did that. I mean, if I went crazy over this so-called debt—and I can't pretend it doesn't piss me off—uh, if I went bananas over this and went up there to mangle people I sure as hell wouldn't be in shape to do my goddamn work back here a few hours later, now would I?"

Hulera shrugged and pursed his lips, narrowed his eyes at Cole.

"You mind coming to the station with us, Cole?" Drummond asked.

"Sorry." Cole said. "Unless you've got a warrant."

"We can get one by tomorrow morning," Hulera said.

The lights dimmed as Catz's set began. All three of them had to shout to overcome the rock'n'roar.

Cole was glad the light was poor, so Drummond couldn't see his face clearly. He felt sure the growing terror he felt—nothing frightened him more than the prospect of being locked up—was reflected somewhere in his face.

"You'll have to get a warrant," Cole said. "I've got a bar to run and with that debt hanging over my head I'm gonna stay here and make sure it makes as much money as possible, you can be *damn* sure—"

"That's a pretty poor excuse, pal," Hulera said, leaning forward, his voice self-consciously steely.

"Damn it, Hulera, that's a *good* excuse," Drummond shouted at the other man. He nodded to Cole. "Tomorrow." And he led the frowning Hulera out of the bar.

Cole fixed himself a drink.

"This is suspicious behavior," Cole murmured to himself, sipping, looking after the cops. "I should have gone with 'em. Maybe I should go after 'em and answer their questions. What the hell."

His attention was snagged by a figure reflected in the neon-sprayed front window with its blinking COORS sign—a shadowy figure superimposed over reflections of people inside the bar. It was visible only when the sign blinked from yellow to red. Red: It was City, standing there in trench coat, slouch hat, and mirrorshades.

Cole looked around. City was nowhere near (unless macrocosmically). The reflection was all there was of him. A reflection with no one to cast it. City was looking right at him and shaking his head. "You mean," Cole mouthed, "about the cops? Should I go and talk to them?"

City shook his head, and blinked out and was gone.

Cole went back to work. When the next set ended, Catz came to him at the bar. "I heard City's voice in the stage monitors," Catz said. "He spoke to me."

Cole's heart went cold. "He's got something else for us to do. . . ."

She nodded. "He said for you to go to the pay phone."

"Why?" Cole threw down his polishing rag. "It was enough tonight. I can't take any more. Uh-uh. It was enough for ten *years.*"

But he went to the phone.

At the nonscreen wall phone he picked up the receiver, plugged most of the disco-throb out with one finger in the other ear, and listened. Immediately, heard sharply over the dial tone, was City's voice: "Don't talk to the police at all if you can avoid it. I'll try to swing suspicion onto the Tongs, I think. The Triads. Roscoe has your voice on video-tape, from the camera. I was able to block out the picture but I failed to stop the sound recording. So they could match you that way if they got you to the station. . . . Now, go to the First Tongue concert at the Memorial Auditorium. Vigilantes are going to try to break it up because the band won't buckle under to the Mob's Performer's Union. We'll play it by ear and look for opportunities. Go to the south exit and I'll get you in. Go *now.* "

"Hey, look, I'm tired of this play-it-by-ear stuff," Cole began shrilly. "You said nobody'd be hurt but there're—" He lowered his voice, glanced over his shoulder "—there are people *dead* back there at that place and at least two of 'em don't need to be. At *least.* There was no reason to kill that guy with the extinguisher, City, you could've knocked him out, or . . ." Cole's voice trailed off. No sound on the other end but the dial tone. He had the distinct feeling . . . "City?" . . . that City was no longer listening.

He threw the phone's plastic earpiece at the dial, watched it bounce off and fall to swing like an ugly pendulum on its jointed metal cord.

Catz stood beside him, holding his coat. "I already told Bill to take over for you," she said. "My band'll finish without me. Fuck it."

Cole slowly reached for his coat. There were three layers of fear inside him. The first layer was fear that he'd be killed or taken prisoner. The second was fear for his nightclub and, mixed up with that, fear for Catz's sake. The third layer was the terror he felt whenever he recognized that he somehow had no choice when it was time to do as City told him. . . .

He put on his coat and followed Catz out the door.

The south exit of the auditorium was chained shut and there was no one keeping an eye on it. City had opened the two padlocks on the chains, and Cole had only to unwind the chain from the door handles. The door was locked from the inside too, and resisted Cole's tugging. Catz said, "Stand back from it." Cole stood back. He heard a double clicking sound When he tried the door again, it was unlocked.

Cole pushed wide the door; they stepped into the warm, smoky interior. They were in a hall outside the bathrooms. The concrete corridor resonated dully with the bass and percussion of the band booming from the stage on the other side of the wall. . . . They weren't alone. They'd been seen entering.

Punks and *angst rock*ers stood in calculated disarray against both walls. The punks wore self-made clothing, festooned with chains and odds and ends of jewelry, gewgaws, randomly-chosen pin-on buttons; their outfits—similar in style but no two quite alike—were collections of clashing, dissonant clothing parts, all reflecting their dislike for mass-produced clothing and computer-design fashions. The *angst*ers wore mostly uniforms—any sort of uniform would do, but prison uniforms were a big favorite—or hospital in-patient tunics. There was a smattering of rubber clothing, black leather, chrome link, transplast sheathing, and voguer scales. The crowd, smoking cigarettes, pot, and alkaloid sticks, regarded Cole and Catz blandly. But in some expressions Cole read respect: "Somebody got in free," someone snickered. "Slick job rubber-carding that door, slutter."

Thatch-headed punks, faces crudely tattooed with India ink in dollar signs, death's heads, and anarchy symbols, swaggered toward the south exit; the *angst*ers, the glowering, disconsolate type, stood back, hands thrust in pockets and eyes moody beneath their uniformly black-banded foreheads and crewcuts. Punk women, bare breasts bobbing, bondage rings through their nipples catching the light, giggled and inclined their heads toward Cole, " 'E a bit *old* for this, in't 'e?" they asked one another in the traditional apocryphal British accent. Cole inwardly smarted.

Smiling arrogantly, Catz took Cole by the arm and led him off to the right, toward the auditorium entrance nearest the stage. Behind them, punks were calling to friends loitering outside, offering free entry through the breached exit door.

Catz was notorious and might have been recognized if not for the plastic domino mask and diabolic make-up combining to hide most of her face. She wore tights, the cloth over the right breast cut away, brown flight-jacket and black leather pegged pants. Her hair was up in spikes, so that she resembled, on the whole, a portrait painted by a paranoid; it was a punk look, which made her a bit outdated. The punks were mostly over-thirty relics.

They passed along a ghostly, blue-lit corridor, kicking aside plastic pill dispensers, cigarette wrappers, and government-issue hypos, turning left to emerge into the main auditorium. They stood at the edge of the roistering toe-to-heel crowd, a dozen yards from five of the monumental PA speakers, each speaker big enough for two men to climb inside, right of the stage. The heavy-metal thunder washed over them, shook them in sensurround currents and forced them to sway. . . .

Catz moved through this element (the brash roar of an *angst rock* concert is an element to itself, a pocket sea of palpable sound; music one can feel physically, a sonic seduction rattling the joints and air-pressuring the hair to disarray, vibrating teeth to chatter) with the confidence of a falcon through windstormy airs.

Cole glowed with admiration for her.

Like some great beached dragon, the crowd moved in one body, in reptilian ripples, one multicelled massiveness writing under the demanding massage of rock'n'roll medium, its piebald hide—fifty thousand faces blurred one onto the next—vibrant with life as it fed off the prodigious amplification storming rhythmically from the band.

The players were costumed as gnostic holy men, initiate magicians, and alchemists, respectively, in arcanely figured robes of red and black and silver. But the lead singer wore only a burlap loincloth and, on the sweat-glistening skin of his thin chest, a burn-scar brand of The Sign, the cabalistic sign for chaos, the cross whose base becomes a scythe. His cat-eyes (pupil-slit green contact lenses) gleamed with alien intelligence. He wriggled masochistically under lash of bass and drum beat beat beat, moving in a bizarre choreography that was at once spontaneous as a whipsnap and elegantly contrived, each step part of some invocatory urban voodoo rite. . . . In interviews the singer had insisted that First Tongue's instruments spoke in tongues, the First Tongue, the language of pre-Babel times and the language of the angels. It was the only remaining successful occultist rock band, a genre begun almost three decades before by the Blue Öyster Cult.

The singer, whose stage name was Blue Drinker, sang in sibilant mockery:

The six legs of the breathing cadaver
Who invades death's peace with spike of ice
His six tongues in mordant palaver
Speaking the return of an electrical Christ . . .

And just then the light show crackled on. In the tumult of smoke overhanging the audience the lasers stabbed as red and strict-edged as the inevitability of death, interplaying and clashing in a lightning-laced web, pulsing on and off in diabolic code, primary colors, ethereal streaks of hot steel and wires of light: to the music. Always synched to the music, to the first and the last echoing beat of snare drum and to every staccato riff of lead guitar, flaring in exact reference to the wailing strains of the synthesizer, the funeral boom of the bass. The lights were a function of the sound, interconnected with a lag of a thousandth of a second by the backstage computer. The computer sensed, at that climactic moment in the surge of song, that it was time for the holography; the laser rapiers split, refracted, suffused, and formed shape like wood turning on a lathe, conforming to the configurations of the great electromagnetic fields projected from hidden sources in the ceiling.

And the roaring, cheering crowd, whose mesmerized faces were upturned like tossing waves before a storm, beheld a beast big as a naval destroyer. It was a freakish, subhuman thing, a six-legged man who crawled on its armor-striated belly like an arachnid, its huge misshapen head flashing with six eyes of six mystically-attuned colors, its lipless mouth opening to reveal the bars of a city jail from which prisoners peered with hollow eyes. . . .

Gigantic, three-dimensional, solid-seeming, swimming through the smoke given off by the crowd, the thing moved to the precise-but-raging strains of First Tongue, while around it holographic buildings toppled in geysers of dust, crushing the city's denizens who ran shrieking. . . .

The holographic image of the monster moved its scaly man-limbs shrieking . . . to the music (the structured roar from the stage beneath it seeming to hold it in the air, creating it again and again from second to second), reaming through the projected city. And Blue Drinker, his cadaverous face expressing an apotheosis of sorrow, portentously recited a Biblical passage:

"*. . . And I beheld another beast coming up out of the*

earth and he had two horns as a lamb and he spake as a dragon . . ."

The holo beast sprouted two horns and its mouth issued flame.

". . . And he doeth great wonders so that he maketh fire come down from heaven on the earth in the sight of men . . ."

The holo image showed fire raining on the beast and its carnage.

". . . And he causeth all, both small and great, rich and poor, free and bond, to receive a mark in their foreheads . . ."

And the people depicted in the holo image, now on their knees worshipping the flame-spouting beast, were marked with numbers on their foreheads, while on stage, a fluorescent light clicked on over Blue Drinker so that something on his forehead, till now unseen, was revealed: 666.

Catz stamped a foot in delight, and Cole laughed. The number was electrostamped—like an ITF number.

Cole leaned over and shouted in Catz's ear, "Where are the vigilantes we're supposed to be watching? And what the hell do we do if we see them?"

Catz shrugged effusively. Cole couldn't be sure if she was shrugging in answer to him or because she couldn't hear him.

The band thundered on like a phalanx of armored tanks grinding across a battlefield. The melodies were precise and involved, but amplified and toned with an edge that, to the uninitiated, made them sound like a wall of noise. But like an armored vehicle which at first glance seems a bullish mass of metallic aggression and nothing more, the music, closely examined, was made up of many carefully-honed and securely interlocked parts. A great machine of sound.

The vast hall, built to accommodate 55,000, was dominated by the broad dance floor, which was filled almost to the walls that upheld the tiers of bleacher seats. There was a narrow margin around the edge of the dance floor kept clear, by order of the fire marshal, enforced by scores of security guards and bouncers. Here and there fights broke out, bottles were flung, smoke bombs went off, so that the scene looked more than ever like a battlefield.

Under the bleachers three gates were open, leading to the front doors. Out of these passages trooped a small army of men uniformly wearing blue jeans and blue shirts, features melted by nylon hose. Some of them held guns, others were dragging firehoses. *The vigilantes,* Cole realized with a shock. The show had almost made him forget his errand. And the men he'd helped murder . . .

He looked around the fire passage. The security guards abruptly left the scene. As if by prearranged signal.

Shouts and spastic buckling of the outer edge of the crowd showed where the vigilantes began to penetrate. Cole saw the crackle of cattle prods.

Catz led him cautiously around the flank of the panicking crowd, toward the vigs. But they were forced to press against the current as the throng bulged like a startled amoeba, away from the threat at its back and toward the stage and side exits.

People up front, crushed against the stage-facing, climbed frantically onto the platform, their numbers overcoming the stagehands trying to hold them back, while—ignoring the *angst*ers and punks fleeing past them—the band gamely played a tune written by Aaron Dunbar, The Hustler:

God's dead and I want his job
Godfather of the Cosmic Mob!
Everybody
is driven by greed
Everybody
enslaved by need
And only way free of this damned curse—
IS TO OWN THE UNIVERSE!
God's dead and I want his job—

The vigs fired at random into the crowd, just enough to drive it like a herd of fear-maddened cattle toward the stage. . . .

"They're trying to drive the crowd to crush the band!" Catz cried in disbelief.

The band played on, faces set grimly. The music came on like an invisible juggernaut. Blue Drinker danced more, more maniacally. He seemed to be revelling in the chaos created by his enemies.

Catz and Cole sheltered behind a concrete pillar as the audience streamed willy-nilly to the right and left. And the fallen were trampled.

The vigs turned on the firehoses and pressed into the tightening heart of the terrified congregation.

The holo image overhead was altering. . . .

It lowered itself from the region of the metal-raftered ceiling to just above the audience, so close that, even in their panic, they could not ignore it.

It was an image of one of the vigilantes, his back spangled in red, white, and blue stars, strangling Blue Drinker. . . .

City's doing that, Cole thought suddenly.

The vigs looked up, hesitating, truncheons or guns or cattle prods or nozzles in hand.

The audience slowed its flight, and heads tilted back to

take in the projected image overhead—now it was a huge three-dee image of Lance Galveston, the union boss. Most of the crowd recognized him. And Blue Drinker, from onstage, roared with laughter and danced the band on. The great machine of heavymetal rocksound lurched ahead.

The firehoses in the hands of the vigilantes had ceased to gush, and their bearers looked down at them in confusion.

The image of Lance Galveston turned and glared down at the crowd. He was an old man with a seamed face and yellowed eyes. He reached palsied hands to unzip his pants . . . and urinated on the crowd. Behind him holo images of vigilantes laughed and pointed.

And the music, with its subverbal message pounding martially, spurred the crowd on. . . .

Almost as one, the audience turned and, united by City's calculated visual jolt, attacked. The vigilantes fell back, ran helter-skelter to the doors. A few of them turned and fired wildly, but though one or two of the onrushing horde fell, the rest hurdled the fallen and overtook the gunmen, bearing them down and rending them in an orgy of catharsis. Anger long suppressed, unconscious resentment at what the vigs represented, boiled outward. One by one the vigs were overtaken and crushed. . . .

Cole followed Catz out the archway, into the hall, and out the south exit.

The noises of city traffic seemed muted and inconsequential after the bruising storm of sound they left behind.

They ran side by side through the parking lot, dodging cars that swung hysterically along the driveways. Catz began to outdistance Cole as she led him toward a knot of fleeing vigilantes fifty yards off. The night air sang raggedly in Cole's lungs and his ears rang from concert amplification.

The panorama of parked cars jounced in roughed metallic planes as Cole jogged after Catz. He was huffing, his face burning from exertion.

Ahead, on the other side of a dented black Cadillac, three men were piling into the front of a blue Datsun pick-up with a white camper hood over its bed. A '79 model. The truck's lights came on, the engine started.

Running in a crouch, Catz sprinted for the truck's rear. The camper's upper gate was propped open: Probably the vigs had brought others in the back, others they were now deserting. Catz swung easily inside. Out of breath, Cole stumbled after her, climbing awkwardly over the lower tail-gate. He was half inside when the pickup jolted and began to move, nearly throwing him back onto the asphalt. But Catz grabbed his collar and roughly hauled him in. He barked his shin on a tire jack as he tumbled inside, and bit off an angry shout. It was dark in the back of the rumbling truck, but if the men in front looked back they'd probably see the stowaways.

Cole, on hands and aching knees, followed Catz over the cold metal of the pickup's bed to a corner under the cab's back window, where they could hunch down on opposite sides, hidden from the men in front.

Cole had no weapon. He felt about in the darkness for something, and his fingers closed over a metal bar.

Squealing around corners, the pickup trundled rapidly. It was a short trip, maybe five minutes. The tire jack rattled mockingly.

The vehicle slowed, the rattling lessened, the engine rumble became a thrum, and Cole felt the truck pull into a driveway and jerk to a stop. The engine shut off. Cole stiff-ened, waiting, gripping the bar on the floor, careful not to pick it up yet so as not to accidentally bang it on something. He held his breath. *This is insane,* he thought. *Catz is crazy.* The pickup doors slammed, and Cole's head against the rear of the cab ached from the vibration.

Maybe they won't look in the back, he thought.

He heard footsteps moving away from the truck, and he relaxed slightly, feeling safer . . . Until a dark shape at the rear of the truck pointed the blinding beam of a flashlight so it shone directly in Cole's face.

FOH-ur!

COLE TIGHTENED HIS GRIP on the metal bar resting on the truck bed, and waited till the man with the flashlight and gun, moving toward them in a crouch, was rearing over him in the murky confines of the camper, features gargoylish in the flashlight glow illuminating his face from below: And Cole yanked up on the bar, putting his weight into the effort. And shouted as his hand refused to come and he was thrown off balance, falling painfully onto his back. The bar was bolted to the floor; it was a handle to the cover over the transmission sheathing.

There was nothing funny about it, Cole thought—so why was the vigilante laughing?

Cole's right arm ached and he wondered if he'd pulled the joint out of the shoulder socket. The arm would have screamed if it had had its own mouth, when the vigilante twisted it to fling Cole onto his stomach. The man locked Cole's wrists into handcuffs.

Out of the corner of his eye, Cole saw Catz move in a blur. There was a bang, a metallic thumping, and curses from struggling figures on the metal floor.

Face down, Cole could only listen and try to worm out of the way. He smelled gasoline and tire rubber and the vigilante's sweat. He tasted the iron tang of his own dread. The flashlight's beam tilted crazily about the enclosure—and went out.

Catz yelped. The vigilante grunted in something like triumph.

Maybe if I lay here very still they'll forget about me, Cole thought.

The flashlight came on again and was joined by another beam. Another man—or was it a big woman? the voice was high—stood blackened behind the second flashlight source at the rear of the truck, saying, "You jerk, you should have made them come out to you, one at a time, instead of getting in the truck with 'em. You could have been bashed."

He would have been, if I hadn't fucked up, Cole thought.

"Shut up," growled the vigilante beside Cole. The man's breathing was labored and his face was that of a huge fetus, under the nylon, inchoate and unfinished. He was dragging something past Cole.

Dragging Catz. *Like she was a sack of garbage,* Cole thought, tears burning at the corners of his eyes.

Without thinking, compelled by a sudden fury, he rolled onto his back and kicked at the man, catching him in the shins.

"Shit!" the man yelled, staggering back.

Then others climbed into the truck and Cole felt himself roughly lifted, toted by the collar and ankles out of the truck and through the night. He felt seasick. "City . . ." Cole said hoarsely, as strangers bore him feet first up a walk and through a doorway.

"Whud he say?" someone asked behind.

"I think he said, 'Pity!'" someone else said, adding, "Tsk tsk tsk." Cole and Catz were carried into the house. They dumped Catz on a black sofa.

City! But perhaps City's influence was diminished here; this was, after all, Oakland, across the bay and south of San Francisco. It was far from city's heart, and perhaps far from his strength. But they hadn't ridden long in the truck, they wouldn't be far from the Oakland auditorium. And City had helped them there.

They dumped Cole onto the floor, on his belly. He gasped as the impact knocked the air from his lungs. He choked, inhaled raggedly, got his breath back at the price of inhaling a lungful of dust from the green carpet.

Booted feet paraded past his nose and there were short bursts of laughter, longer bursts of anger. "Keep away from the window you bloody asshole!" and "Hey fuck *off*, the neighbors don't give a—" and "Yeah but there's a creepinnit *patrol* car goes by here and those boys haven't—" and "Hey just shut up you guys!"

Catz was left on the couch to his right. Slowly, his arm aching, he rolled onto his left side till he could see the couch. It was a dusty vinyl couch speckled with cigarette burns. From the floor he could make out only Catz's limp right arm and the curve of her hips. For the first time it occurred to him that she might already be dead.

Might be dead.

"Hey look, we gotta wear these masks all night or what?" someone said.

The woman's voice replied, "Naturally, dumbshit, we gotta wear 'em until we get rid of these two. I guess we could blindfold 'em."

"Let's wait to see what Salmon wants."

"Who said that?" the woman demanded.

"Hey-uh-shit, they ain't gonna leave here alive anyway, they may as well see us. No reason we should watch our talk when—"

"Look asshole, anything could happen. Anyway, maybe he'll want to do a ransom trip with 'em which might mean he'd have to release 'em. And then they—"

"Not now that this jerk opened his mouth about Sa—"

"Hey what kind of rubber card are you feeding me? I don't credit that bullshit, we gotta—"

"Hey this's one of those punker girlies!"

"Hey the slutter's got a bare titty!"

Cole was nauseated.

"Hey can we take this one into the bedroom for a few min—"

Cole felt positively sick.

"Look, Salmon ain't transferred nothing into *my* fucking account for three weeks and until he does I'm gonna do—"

Cole sneezed, gagging on dust.

"Hey, we got through. He heard about the weird shit at the auditorium already and he doesn't know what happened with the holo either. . . . Says to find out what we can about them and then take them to see Alcatraz from the fishy point of view." Laughter. "Says leave the masks on for now." Groans. Someone grasped Cole by the handcuffs. He was yanked abruptly upright, biting his tongue to keep from sobbing as the cuffs' metal bit into his wrists and his bruised arm was wrenched. Dizzily, tottering, he looked about him. A sparely furnished tract-home. New but dingy. About thirty of *them,* lounging in doorways, sitting at a wooden dining-room table beside the kitchenette, leaning against the undecorated walls. Two of them standing just in front of him, waiting for a signal, leaning a bit toward him, their muscles tensed. All wearing hose masks, dark patches of moisture over the mouths. All of them with features blurred by the masks as if they had their faces pressed, flattened, against unseen window panes.

Beside him, on the couch, Catz lay with her arms drooping uncuffed. Someone had removed her plastic mask. She was breathing regularly, and a tightness in Cole's chest diminished. *She's alive.*

As he watched, her eyes cracked open. But she lay still, pretending unconsciousness.

Cole looked at the man standing over him. . . .

"Okay," said the woman.

Sure, the first blows hurt. The first five or six. Remembering later he couldn't be sure, but it's likely he wept and tried to run. They held him from behind. After each blow, they asked a question. To his right temple, a *thump* that grew into a hot roar echoing through his head. "It says *Stu Cole* in your wallet and one of the boys knows your club. And we know you don't like what we're trying to do. So how were you gonna fuck us over at that concert?" (Cole didn't reply.)

To his left cheek, a *crunch* that seemed to spread pain like cracks through him, as if he were a man of glass. "What did you have to do with those weird holos and the *angst*er creeps turning on us?" (Cole didn't reply.)

To his mouth, an ugly *whump* and the sensation of blood popped from split lips, spattering his shirtfront. "Why did you get in the truck? You wanted to see where we were meeting?"

"No," Cole said slurrily, spitting blood. His mouth tasted like an oil slicked beach at low tide. "Wrong truck. Looking for a friend's. Panicked." *They'll never card that one,* he thought.

Thunk to his mouth again, a crackle as a tooth loosened, his head ringing. "You expect us to credit that shit? It won't card. Come on, slutter: Whud you get in the truck for, huh?"

Cole didn't reply.

Thud-thud to his solar plexus, twice quickly. All breath left him and he doubled over so sharply he banged his head on his knee.

"I said whudduh*fuck* you doing in our truck?" said the flattened face.

Cole had no breath for an answer. He slid to his knees. The room was filled with luminous purple snow. He squeezed his eyes shut. Shut *tight*.

For a moment, possibly several moments, he seemed to spin in a glittery darkness. Then a sound brought him alert. The sound of Catz screaming. He looked up. They were slapping her.

Slapping her with a bottle.

A woman (Cole could see her figure vaguely through her workshirt—a hefty woman but probably young) was twisting Catz's hair in a gloved fist. And a large man beside her lashed out repeatedly with his boot, catching Catz in the ribs.

"Hey!" Cole yelled. "Whut—uh, what do you want to know?"

"I sorta thought that would bring him back to us," said one of the men, turning from Catz to Cole.

The lights failed.

And as quickly as darkness came it was sundered as sparks shot from empty light sockets and flames erupting from the molding began to slither up the walls.

Dark figures dashed by. Cole was on his knees; he climbed to his feet. There was a clicking sound and the handcuffs fell away from him. "City . . ." said Cole gratefully, through bloodied lips.

Fragments of the vigs' confused talk came to him as he fumbled toward Catz. . . .

"Whatzuh—"

"Whoze doin' the—"

"Shit maybe it's—"

"Christ I can't see a damn—"

"Could be friends of—"

"Fucking fire, let's get—"

"Looks like uh 'lectric fire—"

"Hell, leave 'em here to—"

"No take 'em with—"

Cole tried to lift Catz; pain shot up his arm, his eyes dimmed. He dropped her back on the sofa. The darkness became dense with smoke. Someone pushed him down as they ran past: He fell onto his right side. The flames climbed higher, heat sucked moisture from his cheeks. The room was lit with uneven flickering, darkness lanced with vivid red and blue. Most of the vigs had gone. Two more running, coughing, out the side door. "Catz—hey—" Cole said, his choking throat raw with smoke, pulling at her arm. She didn't move. "Catz, City set the fucking house on fire to get us out—we gotta get out or we burn!" His words were blurred with the blood in his mouth.

She moaned and shrank from him. She began to cough, her eyes opened wide. She clapped a hand over her mouth. Cole helped her to her feet. His eyes bled tears from smoke, flames licked at his heels, sweat dripped and quickly evaporated. They moved unsteadily toward the door—a rectangle of sickly yellow obscured by smoke, wavering in the heat. Catz's hand disengaged from his and (taking this to mean she felt she could follow on her own) Cole surged forward as the proximity of flames brought renewed energy—the strength of terror.

He assumed that Catz was right behind him.

He ran through a dimmed kitchenette, out the open side door, sprinting for cover behind the bushes, gasping in the clean cool air. Two trucks were leaving from the front of the house. Someone ran by, shouting, on the driveway.

Men were piling into a sedan. A group of black people stood in a cluster on the sidewalk watching impassively.

Cole looked desperately about him. Catz was not there. "Catz!" he yelled hoarsely, as he moved like an automaton back toward the house.

Two men emerged from the front door. carrying something between them. Cole stepped to the concealment of a corner of a garage, and watched. And he could tell by the outline of the figure they carried—slung but resisting, between them—that it was Catz. He ducked back as they carried her into the garage.

He coughed. He looked numbly around for a weapon. But then a pair of headlights shot from the garage's open port, followed by the snarl of an engine starting. A blue sedan rolled onto the driveway, onto the street, turned— and carried Catz away from him.

"You're *sure*, huh?" Cole asked the lined face of the black motel manager.

"Sure I'm sure. The TV works jus' fine," the man replied. "What you so fired up about watching TV foh? You oughta see a doctor you ask me, son. Hell your face looks like somebody run 'er over with a truck. You want me to get you some banda—"

"No!" Cole shouted. The man looked startled and wary; Cole made an effort. "No—in a hurry. Friend of mine's on the late news. Promised I'd watch. I'll get cleaned up right after. Ran into a lamppost."

"Can't let you in there just to watch TV. Gotta charge you for the room no matter how short a time you stay," said the manager, shrugging.

"Yeah, yeah okay. . . ."

The old man took Cole's card and punched it into the

terminal. He glanced at the results on the small screen, nodded faintly, and handed the card back.

Cole stood impatiently shifting his weight from foot to foot until the slow-moving old man brought the keys. Number seven.

Cole grabbed the keys and ran out the door. Side aching (wondering if his ribs were cracked), lip beginning to bleed again, he checked the door numbers till he found *seven,* and hastily twisted the key in the lock. It opened on the first try and he sighed with relief as he pushed the door open. He plunged into the musty dark room, leaving the keys dangling in the open door. He went single-mindedly to the TV set, slid his Interfund card neatly into its slot, and the TV blinked on.

"City!" Cole screamed at it. "Come on, talk to me!"

A blank screen buzzed back at him.

"I know you're listening!" Cole shouted. "Goddamnit, come *on!*"

The blue-white rectangle flickered tantalizingly. But . . . nothing.

"City! Show up and talk or I leave town! I'll leave and spill everything to the fucking *National Enquirer!"*

And Cole waited.

Nothing.

He flipped through the channels. News, porn, game-shows, *Capital Punishment Review, The Children's Discipline Hour starring James Bondage*—and no City. He returned to the blank channel.

Catz.

Cole waited, fists balling, wondering where they'd taken her. In the distance fire engines sounded, going to the burning house three blocks north.

Cole stood swaying, tense and harried as a TV antenna in a high wind.

"*City!*" Cole wailed, his voice getting hoarse.

And then, a dark two-dimensional bust on the screen, features sullen and stark.

"City . . . Why didn't you get her away from them? Why didn't you stop their car?"

"I've decided against employing the woman's services."

"What? Why?"

"She is disloyal."

"Are you—*What?* She talked *me* into going tonight! She's done everything you wanted her to—"

"No . . . I can feel her inside. Her thinking. She mistrusts me. She is going along because of you. She thinks she is protecting you. I don't want her with you. *I* can protect you."

"She's protecting me? From what?"

City did not reply.

"Well get her *out.*" Cole said, his jaws bunched.

"No."

Cole's mouth dropped open. He stared uncomprehendingly at the screen. "No." He repeated, shaking his head. "No? Look, you don't have to, um, employ her anymore. Just get her out alive and let her . . . let her leave."

"I can't. I haven't got the power now. I've used too much power tonight. I'm weak."

And the image was gone.

"You liar. Fucking goddamn *liar,*" Cole said to the blank screen. He turned, walked out the door, went to the phone booth. And called a taxi.

But Cole waited till the next day to move. All night he'd paced his apartment, smoking cigar after cigar until his mouth tasted like a diesel smokestack and the room sank into stale gloom. Half a dozen times he went to the phone to call Bill, thinking of hiring muscle to help free Catz. Each time he'd walk to the phone to mechanically begin the play of fingers over the buttons, and just as it began to signal the other end, he'd cut the connection. Because if City were really determined to keep Catz out of the way, then he might stop Cole from getting to her. He might stop Cole, at night.

During the day, City could not stop him.

"Maybe they're doing it to her right now," Cole would say to himself. "Beating her."

At two A.M. he murmured, "Maybe they're beating her and raping her."

At three he sputtered, his voice higher than on the previous occasions, "Maybe they're *cutting* her."

At four he wept.

At five he began to drink. Cole didn't drink often, but when he did he went at it with a vengeance. *With a vengeance*—the expression is appropriate: His drinking was always done in rage against someone. As if numbing himself somehow helped to materially erase his enemies from the world.

At seven he was stumbling and sick. Still, he tried to choke down another gin-and-tonic. He couldn't make it to the bathroom, so he had to throw up in the kitchen sink.

He bent shaking over the soiled porcelain, coughing her name, thinking: *God help me, I've fallen for her.*

After a while his head cleared enough so that he could brew coffee. His hand trembled, and he burned himself with hot water slopped from the pot. He drank four cups of coffee; when he lifted his arm, he winced at the neuralgia coursing the bruised flesh.

Caffeine's fight with alcohol produced a headache that rang like a prizefight bell. Hastily he changed his clothes; he washed, carefully dabbing at the cuts on his face. After the first glimpse, he tried to keep from looking at himself in the mirror.

Then he called Salmon.

"Mr. Salmon likes to see who he's talking to," said the secretary. Just the voice. Sounded like an old woman.

"Sorry. Uh—my screen's entirely gone out, both ends. Mr. Salmon knows why. I can't see him either, if that's any comfort. But you tell him it's Stu Cole and it's about his boys at the concert." They put him on hold for twenty minutes.

Thinking, *Maybe they're on their way here.* There was a pistol hidden in his closet, in the shoebox on the floor.

He went to the window. The street looked normal. Posters on the brick walls overlapping like stickers on a world traveler's bag. Mexican children playing on one side of the street; on the other side, a group of black kids walking along singing.

A pimp stood with a patron at the fund transfer booth on the corner.

"Well? Cole?" Salmon's voice, from the phone.

Cole turned from the window and ran back to the phone. Out of habit he stared at the screen as he conversed, though it was blank. "Salmon? Listen, you don't know me—or we haven't met, anyway, but—"

"I know who you are. Now what the hell do you want?"

"I know who you work for and who the vigs work for. And they've got someone and I think, by now, you know who I mean." Distantly, Cole was aware that someone was coming up the apartment building's steps.

"You're pretty darned fouled up, pal. We're investigating the vigilantes and I can tell you that we'll soon—"

"Hey *cut the farce!*" Cole shouted, each syllable sticking a needle through his temples.

There was a momentary silence. "Salmon? You there?

You still with me?"

"Yes . . . Look, Mr. Cole, if you'll explain what it is you want of me I'd be glad to—"

"Hey slutter, don't fake me a rubber card. If you think—" Cole stopped short, listening closely to the footsteps pounding up the stairs. There were several sets of feet moving with unusual urgency.

"Fuck *you*, Salmon!" Cole yelled at the screen, running to the closet. He yanked open the closet door as someone kicked the front door in. The key-locks broke but, judging from the rattling and someone's curse, the chain held. There was another thud as someone hit the door again. Cole dug through the shoebox on the closet floor . . . found the gun, and brought it up just as the man with the hose mask over his face turned, framed by the photos of the city on the living room wall, to face Cole.

Both Cole and the intruder held guns.

But Cole's gun was raised; the other man gripped his low at his right side.

"I'm a good shot," Cole lied, "and I've got a bead on your chest. So freeze. And if your friends come in I'll shoot you." The suggestion of movement behind the man ceased.

The man froze, wrapped face glaring eyelessly at Cole.

"Look—uh—" Cole hoped the man didn't notice his hand shaking. "Uh—I can take out a loan on the club, get some credit together, we'll deal. What do you say? Whoever's in charge, uh—tell 'em I'll pay you to let her go."

"Why don't you call the police?" The distorted lips moved like slugs beneath the pink veneer.

"Very funny," Cole said, scowling against the pain in his head. "The cops are yours."

"Cred-rating is you couldn't get enough money for us to take a chance on letting her live. We thought of that. Some-

one upstairs is gonna talk *real serious* to her tonight, and
then we'll send her back to you in the mail. It'll take four
deliveries."

Someone behind the man laughed. He straightened, as
if encouraged by this, and his hands tightened on the gun
pressed against the right leg of his jeans.

I should kill him, Cole thought. *But how much more killing
can I get away with?*

"Tell me where she is and I won't kill you. That's *all.*"
Cole said.

"Why don't you come and get her? She's right where you
last saw her."

"I last saw her—in the street. In a car." Cole's arm was
beginning to ache from holding the gun; he held it clasped
in both hands, out rigidly at arm's length.

"The fire trucks got there right away. Station's near. Fire
wasn't bad. Whole back of the house isn't hurt. We got stuff
stored there, so we just went back. She's there . . . We got
out before the Oakland cops got there and went back five
minutes after they took off. Simple as that."

"They're not on the payroll, the Oakland cops?" Cole
asked casually.

"Idiot!" someone hissed.

Good information. Could be useful: no allegiance from
the Oakland cops. But then why did they meet in Oakland?
Maybe in the Oakland slums no one really cared what their
neighbors were up to.

"Okay," Cole said. "Back out into the hall; drop your gun
first." The gun dropped to the floor and the vig backed
slowly out of sight around the corner of the apartment's
hallway wall. "I've got friends upstairs with guns!" Cole
shouted, lying. "Get the hell out of the building!"

He heard their steps as they descended the stairs. He
knew they wouldn't go far.

When he was sure they'd gone from his floor, he went out a back window, down a fire escape into an enclosed alley, across the alley and through the broken window of a deserted building. He kicked through refuse in the half-light till he found a street exit with its door hanging half off its hinges. Then he was out into the street and running.

FIGH-uhv!

QUICKLY. HE BORROWED BILL'S CAR and drove maniacally through the rain, with wild indifference to the slickness of the streets.

The rain came two minutes after he'd set out from his apartment. He'd been drenched when he woke his dazed and rumpled assistant manager and simply demanded the car keys. Bill had been too tired to question.

Cole shifted uncomfortably on the vinyl seat, his rump wet, his shirt sticking to his back. The heater in the Chevy Swift was chugging away, the windows were closed, and the rainwater on his clothing was beginning to steam up, making the interior of the car a hothouse. He could smell his wet hair, and old cigarette ashes from the ashtray. There was a rotten taste of cigar residue on his tongue. His headache had receded, replaced by a malicious burning in his stomach.

The streets glimmered uniformly wet, vitreously black, something membranous and organic in their sheen.

The tired two-door sedan, its dented hood occasionally jumping on the hanger-wire that held its broken clasp

closed, grumbled up onto the freeway on-ramp. He shunt-
ed here and there, eyes on the electronic guidance panels
that lit up on the dash as soon as he entered the freeway.
The traffic guidance systems weren't installed in the city
itself yet, and fewer than half the cars on the road were
adapted, so its use was optional. Cole was groggy from lack
of sleep; his eyes aching, he elected to use the guidance system to get him into Oakland. He switched on the unit and
leaned back, let the steering wheel drive itself. It was still
hard for him to get used to, watching the wheel moving
without his touch, the brake pedal pressing itself down as it
compensated for a car slowing just ahead. . . .

The Swift rattled onto the bridge. In the windy wet
morning the sea opening out from the Bay Bridge was a
vastness of ruffled jade, seeming too ancient and all-encom-
passing to be shackled by the bridge-span; the sea waiting
for the inevitable earthquake and its last laugh at the arti-
fices of civilization.

Cole looked over his shoulder. Through a veil of fog the
city rose in pearly towers, which in this mysterious perspective seemed the peaked ramparts of an exotic foreign city.
Cole's heart ached when he made out the fang of the Pyramid Building, remembering a man spasming his life away
on the floor.

Looking ahead at the approaching clutter of Berkeley
and Oakland, Cole leaned back. He let his hand rest on the
butt of the pistol in his coat pocket. "And do *what?*" he
asked himself. "Going to threaten to shoot them all? But
who could I have brought to help? Maybe the Oakland
police . . . but no, I'd have to explain . . . still, if it's the only
way to get her out . . ."

The car's engine coughed once, as if to say *Stop talking to
yourself, Cole, it's embarrassing me.*

"No one else to talk to," Cole said.

Talking to yourself is a bad habit, the car said in rumbles and whirs, *so talk to me instead.*

"Oh *shit!*" Cole said. His weariness had him close to hallucination. Also—worrying about Catz, trying to accept what he'd seen. The men killed. Coping with this had brought him near a certain verge, an edge he'd not seen since he'd overdosed on drugs as a young man.

Oh shit, I don't want to go crazy, Cole thought. But then it occurred to him that it might not be entirely his doing. City couldn't stop Cole in the daytime, but he could contact him. A car is just a moving part of a city, after all, like a blood cell in a man's veins. And through the car . . . *Talk to me instead.*

"No," Cole said, and then he laughed at himself.

Relax. Rethink what you're doing, said the whisper of wind over the car, said the snick of pistons.

Is it hallucination or is it City? Cole wondered. *Or both?*

The car had swallowed him. Was carrying him away against his will. Carrying him in its belly to some bleak underground garage where he'd spend a cement eternity. The car had a will of its own—the steering wheel moving by itself. Feeling trapped, melting into the vinyl seat, molded by the compressing windows—

With an angry grunt Cole snapped to sit rigidly upright, shaking himself. He rolled down the side window and let cold air blast his face. With a shudder, the disorientation passed from him. He rolled the window back up, leaving a crack for fresh air, and switched on the radio as a distraction. The radio squawked a hellish multitude of voices, till he tuned in a news program: ". . . at this point becomes not only logical but inevitable that the postal service switch over one hundred percent to mass electronic transmission of printed matter, excluding parcels. The present sixty percent is not efficient. Uniformity is expediency, and certainly we cannot hope to manage a divided postal system properly, so it becomes necessary to require a mandatory installation of data transterminals in every home that expects to receive mail. The advantages far outweigh the disadvantages. Obviously, typing a letter in your home which is instantly transmitted—either as you type or as a unit, depending—"

Cole changed stations. "No more regular mail, huh?" he murmured, sampling stations. "Hell, I *like* opening letters."

In traveling the FM broadcast spectrum he caught the phrase, ". . . vigilantes supposed to . . ." and he dialed back and forth till he found that station again. "But if these men and women are not public servants—and they've been shown to be far worse than the Robin Hoods they'd have us believe they are—then what *are* they? Their appearance at a rock concert last night—and the subsequent carnage—seems very out of place. This reporter is simply not buying the excuse, as relayed by the tape left anonymously at the station, that the concert represented a 'focal point of corruption and sleaziness.' Pretty thin stuff! More solidly we come upon information that the band First Tongue refused to deal with the rock musicians' union, which even children know is run by organized crime. Are the vigilantes, then, a branch of the Mafia?"

"No shit, motherfucker," Cole said.

He switched off the radio as the car left the freeway. The car threatened to park itself unless he took control once more; he was back in an area without electronic guidance.

Cole cut the unit and took the wheel, swinging onto the exit that said *San Pedro Blvd.* He drove for a mile, chewing his lip in spite of the painful split in it. As he neared the block where he'd have to turn to find the vigilantes' safehouse, the bruises they'd inflicted began to ache, to throb as if in warning. "Psychosomatic," he told himself.

There was the street. He turned. His breathing sounded

harsh in his own ears. He drove with his left hand, his right in his coat pocket, sweaty on the smug hardness of the gun butt.

Oakland's population was mostly black, and billboards projecting here and there from the sides of housing projects and tenements depicted smiling black people looking deceptively middle-class, sharing cigarettes or hundred proof St. Ides or dancing to disco. Some of the newer billboards, paneled in thick glass, were restless with moving holos of cheerful young blacks dancing to the advertised radio station.

Black faces, less cheerful than the huge counterparts on the billboards over their heads, regarded him with sullen curiosity from windows and from groups standing outside liquor stores. Cole passed two abandoned homemade evangelical churches, THE HOLY ROCK CHURCH OF JESUS CHRIST OUR LORD IN PRAIER, and THE HARD CORE CHURCH OF JESUS IN GOD'S PURE BLESSING. Cole smiled. The smile hardened into a grimace when he saw the motel in which he'd spoken to City. "City . . ." Cole whispered. "Sleep . . . or help me."

And there was the house. Two black boys with conked hair stood on the broken sidewalk nearby, looking at the one-story house's charred front, the mournful sockets of its windows. Cole drove past the house, his heart pumping faster than the Chevy's pistons. He pulled up half a block down, in front of another liquor store. *She's back there,* he thought feverishly. *I'm near her.*

He sat in the car, shaking.

Quickly, he thought. Fast.

And he was climbing from the car, hand on the gun in his pocket, slamming the door with his left hand, turning back toward the house.

What could he do? But he went on, walking in the damp shadow of a moldering hotel. Maybe he could tell the

Oakland police there was a kidnapping going on in there and they'd break in—but no, they'd move Catz out at the first sign of cops.

There was nothing left but to try to sneak in from the side or the back, maybe grab someone from behind, hold a gun to their heads and demand Catz in exchange. That sort of thing worked on TV.

Suicide. But he kept walking.

When he was still ten yards off, he stopped, seeing something anomalous in a narrow, broken-glass-littered walkway between two tall tenements. He stared. He stared at himself, and Cole smiled back.

The figure was wearing different clothing, but it was unmistakably himself . . . excepting its peculiar expression. The term *doppelgänger* came to mind. Cole looked to either side, up and down the street. No one was looking. He stepped into the narrow way. His eyes locked on the image as if he expected it to vanish like a mirage as he neared.

Cole walked gingerly forward, stepping over lumps of dogshit and sodden cardboard. He came within five feet of the apparition. It didn't vanish. It smiled back at him, seeming amused. But at this distance he could see through it. It was translucent, like a poor holograph.

"I thought I left that shit back in the car when I opened the window," Cole said. But he didn't *feel* like he was hallucinating. The thing was there in front of him, vague but unwavering, as much a part of the 'scape as chimney smoke.

The ghost (for so he thought of it) laughed. Cole had the impression that the ghost was laughing robustly, but the voice—unquestionably his own—came to him as a hoarse whisper, "Cole ol' boy you should see your face. But of course you *will*, when our perspectives are reversed."

The thing laughed madly. Cole reached out and

brushed the flaking paint of the wooden wall beside him to get in touch with something tangible. *If it's a hallucination,* he thought, *it should appear no matter where I look.* So he turned to stare at the grey-painted wall, looking for the mirage of himself in the scallop-patterns of dust on the siding. The image did not appear there. When he turned back to look down the alley, the figure was there. There only. Cole experienced, then, a cold rush of *déjà vu,* which in passing swept away his disbelief. Suddenly the scene seemed right and proper. Inevitable.

"It's strange," said the see-through Cole, one hand on its lapel. "But I remember clearly everything you're thinking now—about looking at the wall to see if you hallucinate me there, and the *déjà vu,* and it's more as if I'm experiencing it myself, in remembering, but—but slightly removed from it, like in a dream. Y'know?"

Cole nodded numbly. He knew.

"In fact," his *doppelgänger* went on, "I remember what I'm saying to you *now*—I hear it as a sort of pre-echo just before I say it. Which is strange since I'm talking about the phenomenon . . . I mean . . ." He giggled and his eyes were wide, and at least half-insane. "I mean . . . I knew I was going to say just what I'm saying now since I experienced it before as *you* . . . when I was looking at *me* here, from the you that you are now, and I was going to—well, when I came here to meet you, to warn you, I planned to try and deliberately say something different than what I'm saying now, but here I am saying 'try and deliberately say something different than what I'm saying now' which I'd intended to alter, since I knew, having been *you* hearing it, what I'd say—I mean, this is a strange and maddening sort of circuit, isn't it? Deliciously fucked up. But *you* aren't mad, Cole; *I'm* quite real. I'm even, uh, *solid*—but not in your world. See, man, I exist only fractionally in your world. I'm physically solid *here*, in the dimension of absolute-fact-of-urban-being, but from your—"

"You said something about a warning?"

"Oh, yeah—I remember your asking me that. I mean, I remember when you—when we—when I was you, and I got impatient and asked me that—"

"Never mind!" Cole said.

"That's exactly what you said!" The apparition giggled. " 'Never mind!' you said! Yes, just after I said 'got impatient and asked me that—' "

"Look," Cole said desperately, experiencing rush after rush of *déjà vu*, "tell me what it is—the warning—"

But somehow, as the ghost nodded and gave him the message it had come to give, every one of its words was expected, and fell into place:

"Cole—don't go into the house. I'm here to tell you that. You're at a crossroads in time and I had to come and direct you the right way. Which seems silly since I've already gone *through* it when I was you and I *know* what route you'll choose . . . but then, it's true that I took that fork, that particular option, because I came and warned you. Me. You? De*licious*ly fucked up, the paradox. I *think* 'paradox' is the word. . . ."

"But besides the risk . . . *why* shouldn't I go into the vigs' house?" Cole demanded, looking with increasing horror on the contorting, childlike expression on his face. His dead face?

"Because—ha-*heh!*—uh. Mmm. Well, think about it (I remember saying that): You were tired this morning; otherwise you would have questioned that vigilante's giving in so easily with the information as to where Catz supposedly was. He obviously wanted you to come here. They don't take chances like that, stupid. They moved their headquarters, split it into three places, in fact. There's three men with guns sitting in there waiting for you. To kill you."

Cole was not surprised. *Idiot,* he thought. "But goddamnit where's *Catz?* And what's going to happen to us?
And how did I get like you? And anyway—"

"Look, I'll tell you where Catz is," the ghost interrupted,
smirking. "But I can't tell you the rest because I *didn't,*
when you were me. I remember I didn't, so I can't. Isn't
that just deliciously—"

"Then where the fuck *is* she?"

"In Berkeley, thirtyfourtwennytwo Fourth, just off University. There are four of them playing cards. She's locked
in a closet. They don't expect you but they're armed. I'd
tell you to get help, but you won't, as I remember, because
you're frantic, oh but I can't tell you because—"

Cole turned his back on himself and ran from the walkway as the ghost called after him:

"I *knew* you were gonna walk off after I said 'I can't tell
you because . . .'"

He ran back to his car.

He drove as fast as he could and still survive, interesting a
CHiPS patrol car, which he lost coming off the exit in
Berkeley. He was driving furiously, honking continuously to
warn pedestrians, cutting through back alleys of the green,
residential section of Berkeley.

He shot up the gravel alley, narrowly missing a boy on a
bike who swerved and bounced off a fence. Cole swung the
car, tires squealing, onto University. He ran a red light at
Third, turned without signalling onto Fourth, barreling up
the quiet street at forty-five mph, his eyes sifting house
numbers. He was speeding to keep ahead of his terror. It
was a terror of the implications of what had happened; it
was a terror of his own fury.

Quickly.

And there was the house: red-trimmed stucco, pseudo-Spanish Style, with a dying lawn flanked by eucalyptus trees. A blue Buick sedan in the driveway. He pulled up to the right but didn't bother to park the car, leaving it idling in the middle of the street. Afraid to stop and think, he launched himself from the car and plunged across the street to the house. The sun was out in the south side of the bay area, and a tongue of photon warmth touched his bald spot. Smells of eucalyptus leaves, hamburger cooking.

Quickly.

He ran around back, hoping no one looked out a window. A bleak back yard with the rusting hulk of an old Volks in a leaning wooden garage. *Never mind, hurry. Hurry.*

He ran up the steps onto the back porch. The cement steps weren't loud but there was a sound strident as a gunshot when he kicked open the screen door. Tugging the gun from his pocket *(should have had it out by now, stupid)*, he glared around. Someone was just looking up from the stove (and the man seemed to be moving very slowly, as sluggishly as a slow-motion football recap—it was as if Cole had worked himself into a frenzy of haste till he was actually moving and thinking in time-frames noticeably faster than the others), and Cole dashed at him, pointing the gun at the man's face, squeezing the trigger. Almost as soon as the gun had gone off—and Cole was distantly aware that the man was crumpling with eyes crossed to ogle the bullet hole drilled neatly between them—Cole was charging into the next room, firing at the three men who rose startled, moving slowly, their mouths forming words that did not have time to escape their throats before Cole shot them. He was so close it would have been hard to miss. Still, the man on the far left was hit only in the shoulder, and spun as he fell to roll half behind a deep wooden bookcase. He was clawing in his coat for a gun. And Cole's inertia caught

up with him. He seemed to be slowing, the vigilantes speeding up, two of them dying, writhing in normal timeflow,
one now aiming his gun. Cole flung himself to the left,
moving with difficulty now, as if through syrup. He hit the
floor as the vig's bullet smashed the window behind. Cole
had landed on his sore arm, and the pain made it hard to
operate the gun: The limb was all but useless. Someone was
coming in the front door. It swung open, admitting two
burly men, one black and one a dark-haired caucasian in
sunglasses. Drawing guns.

The closet door burst open and Catz stumbled out,
blinking; she dived immediately for a gun dropped by one
of the men lying beside the overturned card table. The
room was sore with grey gunsmoke and once more the man
by the bookcase fired, again missing Cole—the man's
wound ruined his aim. Cole fought to control his damaged
arm, lost his gun in a whirl of confusion and exhaustion.
Catz was kneeling—firing at him? No, firing past his shoulder, at the two men coming across the room. And one of
them got off a shot that slammed through the wooden
bookcase and mistakenly nailed the wounded vigilante.

Pistol detonations shook the room and the two incom-
ing vigs fell. One—wounded in the leg—dropped his gun
and swore as he jerked up to stand on his good leg, and
turned away to hobble hurriedly out the front door.

Cole stared at Catz. She looked ghastly. Pale, her face
smeared with blood, her right eye blackened, her hair matted, her hands still clasping the gun, shaking. She was on
her knees, her face held shock and horror and triumph,
three emotions in three seconds. Then she let the gun fall.
Cole doubled over, dry-heaving, quivering with the sudden
release of tension.

She helped him to stand, and together they staggered
out the back door, down the steps, into the fresher air. They

hurried to the car. Police sirens howled near; people in neighboring doorways squinted at them through the intensifying sunlight.

Cole got in the driver's seat, let Catz press him slowly aside. He deferred to her greater composure: she took the wheel and he leaned against the door frame, dozing as she drove away, tiredly thinking: *Hope to God we get over the bridge and ditch the car before the cops get our license number from the neighbors.*

Apparently no one played ball with the police. Without difficulty they got to the San Francisco apartment of Catz's bassplayer, who was out of town for a few days.

There, they slept in each other's arms.

"I was working on breaking out for hours. Had the ropes off, no sweat. But I couldn't decide when to kick the door down," Catz said. "I was waiting for them to go to sleep."

"I figured," Cole said. The subject made him uncomfortable.

They were sitting in a streetcorner espresso shop. The sun was trembling on the top of a skyscraper; the city trembled on the verge of dusk. They'd slept most of the day on the lumpy mattress in the Castro street apartment, awakening almost simultaneously two hours before to discover that they still lay in each other's arms. They'd never been physically close. And while Catz—to Cole's amazement—lingered there, holding him close, Cole was embarrassed. And his arm fell asleep. But thinking back on it now, he glowed inside.

They'd cleaned up, tended their hurts as best they could, breakfasted on rolls, and come here.

Now, in the bluing light angling through the dusty plate glass beside the cup-cluttered wooden table, Catz's profile was battered but impressive. She sat with her elbow on the table, her angular chin in her hand, her slightly hooked nose sharply outlined against the shadows to her left, her sunken eyes inward-turning—bruises became her nicely, Cole decided, like an *angst rock*er's histrionic makeup. She wore a flat-black wide-lapelled short-jacket, her small up-lifted breasts bare.

Cole's eyes lingered over the scars on her breasts.

Her expression was one of majestic disdain, and her black-painted fingernails and black lipstick gave the pose a certain authority.

They'd been quiet for too long. Cole was aware of a growing unease between them. He sipped his cappuccino for something to do, and tried to seem confident and care-free, like Catz. He didn't want to talk about what had happened that morning. But nothing else came to mind, and he had to say *something*. Anything to distract from the pressure, the expectancy burgeoning between them.

Something's going to happen, Cole thought.

"Uhh—hey, you know, I can't seem to—" he began, stumbling over words, "can't seem to—to remember the faces of the guys we saw—the ones this morning. . . . I *should*—I mean, they're the first we've seen without their stupid masks. But—it's funny, it was like I'd been building up momentum all morning, going faster and faster, trying to find you, and—it was just all a blur. I can't remember them. They might as well have had their masks on because their faces were just pink blurs to me . . . which is, I don't know, *rotten* somehow. Because if you're gonna—" he lowered his voice, "*waste* somebody, you, uh, oughta at least see their faces. Morally, I—"

"I feel the opposite," she said, dismissing his premise with a faint shake of her head. She spoke without removing her eyes from the street scene. "They wore their masks till they trussed me up and left me in that closet all night. So I never saw them, and I wasn't looking carefully at them when we . . . this morning. But I don't want to *know* what they looked like. I don't want to remember that."

"I don't ever want to touch a gun again," Cole said.

Catz shrugged. "Tell me how you found me."

"I told you at breakfast."

"I was all blurry then. I don't think I got it right."

"Okay . . ." So, watching Broadway clowning outside, his eyes straying up and down the increasingly crowded avenue, Cole told her about the men who'd come to his apartment and the warning from the *doppelgänger.*

When he'd finished, she nodded somberly.

Cole laughed. "Aren't you going to say, 'You're crazy! The ghost was a hallucination!'?"

She looked at him with mild surprise. "No. Why should I? You found me, didn't you? How else could you have done it? It must be true. Anyway, I'm used to things like that. To me"—she waved her hand toward the window—"this world is translucent. Sometimes I can see beyond it . . . I'm not picking up much this morning. But last night I could feel you coming to get me. I wasn't sure *when,* but I knew you were on your way."

Cole wondered then whether she was snagging stray thoughts from him now. He reddened, and tried to read her expression. He'd been visualizing the two of them making love. She gazed out the window, one hand tapping the rim of her small espresso cup. No, she'd said she wasn't picking up much today, Cole decided with relief. Her gift came and went.

A crash behind the counter to Cole's left . . . A waiter said, "Fuck!" bending to scoop broken glass. The place was becoming hectic, the evening crowds had almost magically appeared. The steamed-milk pumps—elaborately archaic contrivances of chromium and polished wood—hissed foamy-white into coffees, and a woman with short orange-and-blue streaked hair accepted Interfund cards, which she punched with unthinking efficiency into a terminal. "Thank you," she said, glancing at the readout. "Thank you," in a monotone. "Thank you," handing back a card. "Thank you," inserting a card, punching card, readout, handing it back. "Thank you . . . thank you . . . thank you . . ."

The narrow room's tables were crowded with *angst rock-*ers from the new Deaf Club (which was just up the neon-boisterous street) and S&M voguers with their crouching limpid-eyed slaves on leashes, endangered species coats festooned with gold-plated imitation credit cards.

Outside, *angst*ers, voguers, a few dour Chinese, and tourists intermixed. Earthers in berets, braids, jeans patched with leather, and rhinestone sunsigns, sold pot or return-to-nature papers. "Why are they living in the city if they want to return to nature?" Cole murmured.

A group of *angst*ers in prison uniforms marched by, laughing. One of them lagged behind the others, slowed by a miniature ball-and-chain clamped to his right ankle.

Cole glanced at Catz. The tension was growing between them again. She put on a pair of narrow dark glasses and, rather abruptly, stood to stretch. Cole slipped on his old black motorcycle jacket, and they went outside to join the evening.

The sky was purpling; the few stringy clouds were underlined in violet. Against the horizon Coit Tower loomed phallically. They strolled close together through the sifting crowds. A cluster of Japanese tourists took Catz's picture, and she snarled for them as the cameras clicked. They giggled delightedly. Neon and blazing stipples of light bulbs made hallucinogenic trails in Cole's peripheral vision, the overlapping signs layered thickly brilliant. Cole began to relax, feeling *in place.* The glaring signs in the long row of nude-live-sex-bestiality-bondage-on-stage clubs seemed to flash at him in a familiar subverbal code; the signs were arranged in compositional juxtaposition with the gloomy network of trolley wires crisscrossing overhead. Electric buses flared sparks from their runners when they traversed the nexus of wires at an intersection.

Clusters of gulls patted their wings nervously at the city's brows, circling just over the buildings in close swooping circuits like elements in a mobile.

The street's regular denizens—*angst*ers, voguers, earthers, hookers—paraded up and down the crowded walks, displaying themselves in bright plumage, in the distance melting kaleidoscopically into one another; they reminded Cole of Japanese demons.

A laser wrote on the clouds: *Visit . . . us at . . . the Jade Tower. . . leisurely dining . . . for the . . . elegantly jaded . . .*

The tension between them had wound down, and Cole began to feel almost cheerful (blocking from his mind fleeting images of blurred faces erupting in blood, the man with his eyes crossed around the cruelly neat-edged bullet hole).

But when Catz took his hand, he shivered. And when he realized she was leading him to her apartment, his palms began to sweat.

As they reached the bottom of the hill—having threaded Chinatown, its riot of scents, windows displaying intricacies of ivory and jade, and ten thousand pairs of slanted eyes—Catz pulled up short, jerking him back a bit with her arm. He turned to look questioningly at her, trying to conceal his apprehension. But it was she who asked:

"What's the matter, Stu?"

"Nothing," he said glumly, thinking *Oh Christ, she's beginning to pick up my thoughts.*

"No, really."

Cole shrugged excessively. "Uh—I dunno, Catz. I guess I'm worried about City . . . about him calling us . . . it's almost night. And you—look, I told you he wouldn't help me get you away from those creeps."

"I don't care about that. I expected it. In fact, I think he tripped me up somehow when I was following you out, and he arranged things so the vigs would get me. He's right: I *don't* trust him. He's the subconscious of hundreds of thousands of very fallible people, Stu. Do you think the people of this city are totally sane? Not on your life. Underneath each quiet cranium is a nest of snakes. I remember when I was a teenager I overdosed on acid—I was fine till I lost conscious control and didn't know where I was anymore and I started marching around under the direction of my subconscious. And since my subconscious was full of hostility, I started busting things up. . . ."

He stared at her. He had to speak loudly over the *skree* of a streetcar muscling slowly up the steep hill. "Then why did you go along with him? Why did you help us?"

"You know why. City told you," she said gravely, "though you didn't mention that part to me."

Cole was grateful that, in the gathering shadows, she would be unable to see his face reddening.

"Shit, I'm acting like a scared teenager," he mumbled.

She laughed shortly. "It's so cute when you talk to yourself."

There was no scorn in her tone, but Cole was rankled. He looked away, scowling.

"I think you should leave the city," he said. "He might kill you."

"Maybe I'll leave," she said. "I gotta admit . . . I'm scared too. I like to pretend I'm not. But I won't pretend that with you." Her voice was unusually tender. "I—damn, I thought I'd go nuts in that closet last night. They didn't rape me, but I was afraid they would. I just don't want to go through that again. It's stupid. I want to take the band and leave. But you can't stay here. *He* has you . . . too much. Pretty soon you won't have any goddamn free will, Stu. You got to leave too."

Cole shrugged helplessly. "I don't think I can. Not for long. . . . I don't know."

The light changed; the intersection told them to WALK, so they did. They crossed the street, coming at the next corner to a curio shop whose dusty sidewalk-window held a wooden fortunetelling gypsy. It had been in that window, broken, for at least twenty years. As they passed by the window, Catz abruptly went rigid, squeezing Cole's hand convulsively. She stopped, gazing fixedly at the little wooden doll, the time-beaten face of an old crone grinning wickedly at them. "Its head," Catz said raggedly. "It—wasn't looking this way before. But when I walked past, it turned to look at me. I saw it out of the corner of my eye. . . ."

The tiny gypsy face squinted at them maliciously. Cole remembered that, yes, the toy's head had been facing the other way when he'd first glanced at it.

"Maybe . . . its works started up again. Vibrations from cars or something," he suggested without conviction.

Hurrying on, almost dragging him in her haste, she said over her shoulder, "Bullshit! It's City. I feel it. He's watching me. He let me see that as a taunt. A warning. He's coming alive. He's following me." Her voice cracked. "Oh *fuck.*"

They hurried on, down the darkening street. Cole paused near a subway entrance. Waiting impatiently, Catz took off her sunglasses, to eye him questioningly.

"There's a southbound train coming," Cole said, squinting at the ground.

Catz looked faintly amused. "How do you know? You haven't checked out a schedule."

Cole felt a chill. How *had* he known? He looked up at the street corner. "A Mission Street bus is coming."

Catz followed his gaze. Two seconds later an electric bus with its front ensigned MISSION swung around the corner.

Catz looked at him. Cole felt strange. Cold around the edges. And he couldn't feel his feet. He wasn't really cold, it was a warm night—but his feet felt numb. Like they were melting into the asphalt. Cole stamped them till some feeling itched his soles. Then, he looked up. "Now," he said, "a truck is coming around the corner. And a black guy on a Harley after that." And a big yellow delivery truck swung ponderously by, followed closely by a black on a silvery motorcycle.

Catz stared at him in open horror.

That's when the phone in the phone booth beside them rang.

The folding door to the old-fashioned phone booth folded open. The phone fell off the hook to swing, as if beckoning. Mechanically, Cole began to walk to it, reaching for it.

Catz moved quickly, stepping between him and the phone booth, her arms straight out against his chest. "Don't talk to him. You know he's going to be there. Don't—not now. It's him, he's coming alive . . . and he's making you part of him."

Cole was dazed. He spoke musingly to himself, "All the machinery in the world is connected," he murmured, looking around him in growing realization. "In electrical lines, phone connections—like a big electronic webbing. The pipes . . ." He closed his eyes. He could see it there, in the infinite darkness behind his closed eyes, superimposed luminously, bluewhite against the speckled blackness the great endless blueprint of the city's electrical neural channels, the interlinked buildings and the loci, the nexus of the power plant, the—

He snapped his eyes open, startled. An odd sensation on his face. He realized that Catz had slapped him. He allowed her to lead him to the subway entrance. "Come on," she said. "Come *on.*" She drew him by the hand: he followed passively, feeling giddy and dreamy. They descended into bright lights and clean-white tiles. With an Interfund card Catz bought two coded tickets from the wall computer.

Still feeling distant, dreamy, Cole allowed himself to be led into the sleek, stainless BART train. The doors hushed automatically shut behind them and they strolled the worn rugs to seats beside a broad, graffiti-filtered window. The other passengers talked quietly or read newspapers. It was past the commuting hour, there were only a dozen others heading south in this car.

Cole noted these things carefully but with detachment, as if everything around him, passengers and the devices of the train itself, were small but functional elements in the city's vast machined operation.

The train's urban continuum exercised one of its functions: the subway moved out and, feeling a distant pleasure at the procedural perfection of the machine around him, Cole began to count the lights flashing by in the tunnel. And he listened to the rhythmic click of the wheels, the sigh of air pressuring at corners. . . .

A little while later, Cole came suddenly alert from his reverie of endless blueprints and streetplans. He looked about nervously. He felt lost and alone, disoriented—and knew he'd gone beyond City's reach.

He was relieved, finding Catz beside him. She sat with her legs propped up, boot-heels on the back of the seat ahead, smoking a handrolled cigarette.

"You're not supposed to smoke in here," he said, grinning.

She smiled faintly. "So what you gonna do about it, motherfucker?"

His hand slid over hers. Her skin was warm and moist and seemed to adhere to his.

He still tingled a bit around the edges. "Where—uh, where we going?"

"This is that southbound BART you mentioned, baby. It's the one that goes through the new tunnel in the Berkeley hills, y'know? The new one, only been open a month. Goes almost to San Jose. It's a long trip, but . . . it's out of his reach, I think."

Cole nodded. "I felt myself slip away from him. I'm surprised he didn't stop the train. Maybe it would have killed us to do it. Maybe—"

She shook her head. "No, he could have stopped us at the regular stops, just kept the train from moving out. But there's another reason. Like, maybe he knows"—she glanced at him from the corners of her eyes—"that you'll come back."

Cole took a deep breath. "I feel funny."

"You're being weaned."

"What?"

"Nothing. . . . Hey, when you saw all that stuff coming— the traffic, like precognition—was it that duplicate of you? That image you saw in Oakland? Did he tell you?"

Cole shook his head, watching the tunnel lights flash by. The train hummed equably on and on. "No . . . I don't think so. What I saw was like I was looking through somebody else's eyes. Or like seeing around a corner with a periscope. A TV overview. It wasn't seeing ahead in time . . . it was like the buildings became almost . . . transparent."

"I don't go for that shit—"

"I'm not making it up."

"No, I know that. I believe you. I mean—it looks bad.

He's really got you—"

Cole quickly changed the subject. "But what do you think that thing *was* that I saw? That—'duplicate'?"

"*I* don't know," she said miserably. Her cigarette had gone out. She relit it, frowned at black lipstick stains on its butt. "Maybe it was, uh, a projection of you, your own latent abilities. Like your own hunches shown to you in some kind of vision."

It didn't ring true. "Uh-uh. This thing . . . it was more like a ghost."

She laughed nervously. "Well, it couldn't be that. You ain't dead, pal."

"No," he said. But he thought: *I'm not dead yet. But maybe I will be soon. Very soon.*

It rang true.

"I don't know," Cole said, sitting stiffly on the edge of the creaking bed. "Maybe I should go back. I got to go through with it. I got started with him and I sort of . . . committed myself. I feel lonely, away from the city. Jeez, I haven't been out of it in years. I—"

"Yeah, you're scared of being away from dah-dah," Catz said. "But it's something else, too."

She leaned toward him, twined her fingers in his hair. She said softly, "*You*, pal, are nervous about something *else.*"

Cole involuntarily drew back from her. Faintly, he could smell her perspiration, her natural musk. He was intoxicated. But his back was cold and rigid. "Look, why'd we come here?" He gestured at the old Santa Cruz hotel room. The air smelled faintly of mold and the sea. The peeling wallpaper was yellowed, fungal in the corners. The antique brass bed squeaked with their every movement. "Maybe it's best for you to be away from San Francisco. But—not me. I shouldn't be here. I got a club to run, Catz."

"Excuses, ex-cue-sez . . ." she purred.

"Look, I—"

"How long's it been?" she interrupted, going to pains to make the inquiry casual.

"Since what?"

"Don't play coy," she said expressionlessly.

He hesitated. "Couple of years."

She closed her eyes. She smiled. *Therrrrre* it is. I'm getting your wavelength now."

Cole swallowed to hold back an exclamation of alarm. Her gift . . .

"Ah . . ." she said, sharp teeth showing in her smile. "Ah. You were impotent"—Cole twitched at the word—"the last time. It was with a black hooker. You're afraid you're still impotent. You're afraid you're too old for me. You're afraid I'm going to use you in some way because you can't understand why I should really like you." She opened her eyes. "I'll tell you why I like you, Stu. You gave me my first break at your club, shit, years ago, and you knew it was going to take a long time to build up an audience for my sort of act and you lost money on it for a while. But you went ahead anyway because you cared about me and you understood my music and my poetry. You're the only man I know who really understands it. But it ain't just gratitude. I've been 'lectric on you for years." She laughed at his expression. "It's true, Stu. I love you. City was right. The only reason I've gone along with you in this whole thing with him is to protect you."

"Look, don't—I mean, I can't—I'm, uh . . ."

"Shit-city. You've got a couple of love handles and a potbelly. Big deal. I like my men soft, anyway. They're gentler. Look, I see your fears, Stu. Stop trying to hide from me."

Cole felt his cheeks burning. "Don't—hey—"

"But *now* you're getting angry 'cause I'm reading your

mind a little. I can't really help it, when I'm feeling this close to you. But I'll tell you what: If you feel it's an invasion of your privacy, I can adjust away from your, um, mental images, anxiety-pictures, that sort of thing. You can keep those private. Instead I can look to . . . your feelings. Mentally I can experience some of your sensations. Internal and external. It's like a feedback. So, we can be *really close*, Stu."

He blew out his cheeks. "I get the feeling you're trying to sell me something." He stared at the threadbare rug between his feet.

"Maybe so. If it's the only way I can get through to you." She bent near him. Her lips burned against his neck.

And Cole nearly jumped from the bed.

She pulled him gently back, shaking her head sadly. "Hey re*lax*, Stu."

"I *can't.*" He was shaking. The tension between them was at some kind of peak. He felt that he'd retreated inside himself, that he was watching the scene myopically. "I can't get behind it, Catz. Uh—I wouldn't want to disappoint you. You know?"

She rolled up her eyes. "You still don't get it," she said. An unadulterated kindness in her tone made him look up in gratitude. "You can relax, Stu, because I don't expect anything of you. We don't have to make love very much. I just want to hold you and touch you. We don't have to—to *do* much of anything. I just want—" she gestured impatiently. "Well, it'd be without clothes, but not *necessarily* with great, uh, elaboration. See? I don't *need* to have you inside me. If you feel like giving me an orgasm, fine, that's why God gave you fingers and a tongue and me a clitoris. But it doesn't matter. See, turkey, I love you. So it doesn't matter."

Cole expelled a long breath and something inside him relaxed. He felt alive, more aware, buttery with her communion. Without thinking about it, he reached out and turned off the lamplight. The room darkened, but a cool illumination came from the half-shaded window behind them. Enough to see her by; but it was dark enough so he didn't feel self-conscious about his body.

She'd removed her boots and jacket, was sliding out of her pants. Some of the tension resurged as, hands trembling, sweaty fingers slipping on plastic buttons, he undressed, arranging his clothes over the bedpost more neatly than he needed to.

He turned and slid into her arms. It was easy. She was firm but undulating, her skin smooth yet clinging. Another level of relaxation, and another surge of pleasurable electricity coursed through him, and he felt an odd sensation at his groin. He looked down in surprise. His erection was pressing firmly against the dampness of her labia. Her legs entwined his buttocks, and as their lips met she began an invocatory rhythmic pressure, her mons against the shaft of his penis. Their lips passed a shivery current, and he found himself exploring her with his hands—exploring without forethought or self-consciousness.

"You see?" she said gently in his ear, as her fingers skied his back. "All you needed was to relax. Relax enough and you go through into another place, man. Relax enough, and a lotta lovely stuff'll happen . . . Stu. . . ."

It turned out that she was right.

uh-*SIXZZ!*

IN THE MORNING, AS CATZ SLEPT, Cole gazed at himself in the bathroom's smudged full-length mirror. "Not so bad," he said. "Don't look so goddamn bad at all." Humming, he took a shower.

Returning to the hotel bedroom he inhaled nostalgically the perfumes of last night's sex. Catz was dressed, sitting on the edge of the bed. "Come on," she said, tapping her foot impatiently. "Get dressed, Stu. Let's go."

"What are you so frantic about?" Cole asked, throwing a towel at her.

Moodily she fielded the towel, wound it pensively around her hand as she spoke, "I had this weird dream last night. I saw some things. Connected to what I saw, singing, that night City first came into the club. We got to leave the bay area. Go to New York or someplace. . . ."

"Are you crazy?"

"I'm serious."

"Just drop everything and leave."

"Right. The ship is sinking, old boy. You very nearly didn't get out of the city yesterday. He didn't want you to go."

"He could have stopped me."

"He tried to discourage you—but he knew you'd come back. Let's *go!*"

"After all we've done? The fight? I couldn't just ditch it now, Catz."

She shifted about on the bed, examining him. Uncomfortable under that gaze, he went to get dressed. He pulled his clothes on without thinking about it, and had to rebutton his shirt. When he was finished, she said:

"Have you made up your mind?"

"I can't go. I'm sorry." It didn't occur to him to ask himself *why* he couldn't go. A fish can only survive out of water for a minute or two—and it doesn't question its need for its own element.

"What are you anyway? Rooted in one place?" Her outburst was not angry; it was despairing. She sighed, and said, *"Stu*—baby—do you think the vigilantes are going to let you live after yesterday? One of them got away. You killed a handful of the bastards, remember? They're dead. And *you* wasted—"

"O*kay,*" Cole said, wincing.

"They'll kill you. Simple as that."

"They won't find me. City will protect me."

"Maybe. As long as he has a use for you. But listen, you know that he can't control ITF, and ITF is controlled by his enemies—your enemies now—and they'll cut you off from what little money you have. And they'll close your club. And you can't even go back to your apartment. They'd be waiting."

Cole stared at her, dread coming over him as it comes to a man who realizes he's just had his dick shot away. . . .

"Oh Jesus," he said softly. A man without a credit rating was a nonentity. Without his card, his account—social emasculation.

"But—" he began suddenly, his throat tight. "It would be no better in—in another city. I'd have no fucking account *there.*"

"Not at first. But you could build one up. You could stay with me in—I've got an account in Chicago. Saving it up for years. And we could establish credit for you there—I know for a fact that the Mob hasn't got the ITF in Chicago. That city's too wise to organized crime, they took big precautions right at the start."

Cole paced the room, his hands moving near his lips as if trying to say by gestures what his lips could not mold into words. "He—it's not—shit—I think I'd—" He raked shaking fingers through his hair, trying to conceive a rationale for staying, something she'd find valid. Why was it so hard to make her understand? He couldn't leave City. Not now. Maybe he *was* rooted, a plant that would die unless rooted in the peculiar chemical compounds characteristic of its native soil. The concrete and its San Francisco configurations; the asphalt with the sweat blood vomit tears semen of the people who trod it as its mystic fundament; the copper wire, the asphalt, the aluminum scalings; the particular array of towers of glass and steel; the great grey wooden ladies the tourists saw as Victorian houses; the soil of San Francisco. "You're asking me to rip up my identity and transplant it elsewhere. It'd kill me."

Catz played her final card: "You'd rather lose me than City?"

Cole hedged. "It's not fair of you to—"

"Fuck *no,* it's not fair! Tough shit! I love you and they want you dead. They'll kill you. And he'll use you up and spit you out."

"City won't—"

"City is using you!"

"You don't know that!" he shrilled savagely. He turned to

face her. "You can't be *sure!*"

She shook her head. "Why wouldn't he help you when you asked for help to save *me?* And why did he lie about the 'no killing' part?"

A cold resolve took hold of Cole. He raised a hand to her, palm outward, an emphatic gesture. She fell silent, waiting. He said: "I know. I *know*. It's too bad, though. Just too bad. I love you. I love you, Catz. I guess—I *know* he's using me. And I know I love you. But I have no choice. I made my commitment a long time ago. I have to go through with it. I was chosen."

"You make me sick. 'Chosen.' That's the excuse of terrorists and dictators and religious fanatics—always a cover for something really selfish. I know—you're gonna say, 'Catz, you just don't understand.' I understand—and I reject it. I refuse to be used by him. I'm willing to cooperate with the city-minds, when I feel it's right. I have a rapport with some of them. New York and Chi. I've communed with them. They're just as alive as City—your city. They're not as active—but they've got plans. I think they're planning something . . . together. There is a plane where they commune . . . well, anyway, if you—"

"Catz . . ."

"If you think that he's not—"

"Catz."

"What?"

"I said I *know* he's using me. It's an internal thing. Built into me. I *must*. Okay?"

She stared numbly. "No. It's not okay. It's *not* fucking okay. You're going to become part of the Muzak."

"The what?"

"It's the basic difference between us, man. In some ways you're an outsider, a nonconformist or what have you. But you don't *want* to be. You want to belong. You want to click with a community and be a good drone in the hive—"

"*Bull*shit, slutter!"

"Deep down, man, that's what you want. Cred it. That's why you slide into City so easy. You want to identify. Well, I *don't* identify with him—with any mass of people. I'm scared of losing myself in them. I'm almost nothing—*any*body is almost nothing—but what little I am I cherish, and I'm not going to lose it to City. And I can't stand to see it happen to you. Maybe I'm jealous. But I can't stay and watch it. Anyway, I think he'd kill me. Because I'd always be pulling you away from him. . . . Look, as much as things are fragmenting and as heavy as the culty scenes are, all that stuff—the neopuritans, the neopunks—all that's just trendiness. It's really just fadshit. Even *angst rock*. I'm not an *angst rock*er, that's just the convenient label they stick on me. I don't identify with any of that. It's all part of their wallpaper."

"But being a part of City isn't like that. It's a communing, sure, but it's voluntary and natural—"

"No, it's just that he's got you thinking it is."

There was a hard silence between them. She watched him.

"You're wasting your time," he said.

"Yeah. I can see that. It's too late already, with you. . . . Look, I'm going. There's a guy in Chicago who says he'll produce an album for me if I get him a good demo. So we're going into the studio—"

"You want to make records? *Who's* becoming part of the Big Uniformity? You're going to have to sell out to—"

"No. I'll be able to reach more people. I'll preach nonconformity—"

"They'll package your image and make thousands of posters of you. . . . There'll be The Catz Wailen Look."

"Keep the sarcasm in your own account. It don't transfer." She was shaking. "Shit," she said softly.

She went to the bathroom, ran the water in the sink so he wouldn't hear her crying.

Late afternoon. The brink of evening. In prelude, the sky darkening the creviced undersides of the heavy clouds.

Alone in the San Jose airport, Cole watched Catz's Chicago-bound jet matching momentum with air pressure, sliding into the sky. (No, Cole wasn't genuinely alone; but the people around him were more than just strangers— more importantly, they weren't from San Francisco. Not from Cole's city. Aliens.)

Deep in his coat pocket he fingered the slip of paper she'd given him with the Chicago phone number scribbled on it. . . . The whole band had gone with her, their rat-faced bassplayer protesting that he'd paid the rent on his room for the upcoming month. It hadn't been hard for Catz to persuade him to give Cole the key.

It might be that she was wrong: Maybe they hadn't cut off his account entirely. Maybe he still had his club.

"Fat chance," he said aloud.

The jet was absorbed into the low bank of clouds, clouds looming over the airport like some great ominous genie. Catz was gone.

She was gone and he was in San Jose, away from City. He looked around him. Strangers, crowds of strangers. He was utterly alone.

Quelling panic, he turned and trotted to the escalator that said EXIT TO STREET. *BART* STATION.

Cole gazed at the ITF screen in the public booth with a certain satisfaction. ACCOUNT DISSOLVED, it said. Not just ACCOUNT HELD IN LIEN PENDING REMITTANCE. Not merely NO FURTHER CREDIT EXTENDED AT THIS TIME. Not for him. For

Stuart Cole, the seldom used anathema: ACCOUNT DISSOLVED. They saved that one, generally, for convicted terrorists.

"She was right," he said, as he accordioned the booth's door aside and stepped into the street. He stood on the corner of Market and Sutter, in the shadow of an unlit marquee for a "Therapeutic Erotica" theater whose sign proclaimed: DISCIPLINE ADMINISTERED DURING FILMS/ALL CHAIRS EQUIPPED FOR/TRAINED THERAPISTS. "Trained like a donkey in Tijuana," Cole muttered, turning away.

ACCOUNT DISSOLVED . . . The impact of what had happened was beginning to catch up with him.

He walked slowly down the street, every step creasing his chest with pain. The pain that consumed him was the hurt of rejection by an entire society.

"Why don't they just infect you with leprosy?" he wondered aloud.

He passed a derelict snoring in a night-blackened doorway. *Even the drunks,* Cole thought, *have accounts. Or at least Welfare numbers for begging licenses or disability checks. But not me. I'm below them now.*

He came to a phone booth and waited, staring at it. He was not disappointed: The phone began to ring. "City?" he answered, some of the pain sliding from him.

"Benny?" said a Hispanic voice on the other end. "You got the stuff?"

Swearing so fiercely he wasn't sure what words he used, Cole threw the phone down and stalked away. "City . . ." he said. It was almost a sob. He looked around him, fear coiling around rejection.

City was removed from him. Cole felt insulated, blanked from his usual rapport with the urban environment.

City was punishing him.

Maybe that's it for me, for good. Maybe he found someone else, someone better to do the job. He abandoned me for good.

An electric trolley came trundling down the hill from his left, sparking the overhead wires and swaying as it slowed to let off passengers. It resumed speed, and rumbled to within twenty yards of him. It would have difficulty stopping in time, downhill. It was the only way to know, to be sure how City felt now.

Cole ran into the street, feeling cold sweat coming out on his forehead. He was afraid. Yes, very. Afraid of death. But better to be dead than to be insulated, trapped like a lab specimen in a jar. He threw himself flat on the ground in front of the trolley, squeezed his eyes shut, tried to squeeze out the sounds of its squealing wheels with his hands. Its passengers screamed. He could smell the ozone of the trolley's electrical power. The asphalt under his arms shivered with the approaching wheels. Its shadow came over him, adumbration of death.

And then the street erupted.

As Cole was pitched down the hill. Rolling to the right, he caught a glimpse of a massive pipe sprouting from the street, coming between him and the trolley—which crunched into the pipe, rear wheels jumping the tracks as it skewed sideways. Cole caught himself and stopped rolling.

Grinning with ache, favoring his scraped knees, he got to his feet. The streetcar had swiveled, was crosswise in the street, but upright. No one seriously hurt. People were running toward him, their angry faces seeming to precede their bodies; others stood staring at the huge man-thick pipe that had stopped the streetcar two seconds before Cole was to have been crushed.

"Hey—hey what the fuck's the—" shouted the conductor, bearing down on Cole.

A cab swerved from the lane on the other side of the white line, having come up from behind Cole, and turned so its door swung invitingly open on the rider's side. Cole swung inside and the cab lurched off. He sat in the front seat, gasping.

There was no driver.

"City . . ." Cole said softly, tasting the salt of his own absurd tears.

The driverless cab carried him away. *To where?* Cole wondered. Two blocks and the car stopped. Cole turned and examined the Tenderloin district apartment building before him. High, narrow, dirty yellow. Ellis Street was teeming with strangers, but Cole was no longer alone. Closing his eyes, he could feel a helicopter taking off from a roof six blocks south. In the darkness behind his eyelids he could see the cars of commuters on the freeways north and south, each car moving with an eerily even pacing, the same distance apart and moving at the same speed, as if carried along on an invisible current. As if, again, the cars were red blood cells drawn by the current of a bloodstream. And he could feel a BART train passing under his feet, the pipes gushing and burbling around the subway tunnels; the crackling electrical strength in the thousands of miles of wire interlacing; he could smell torrents of sewage pumping and the sickly exhaust of thousands of combustion engines commingling gases with hundreds of thousands of foodcooking wafts. It was all perfume to Cole.

He opened his eyes and went upstairs.

He found the apartment by looking through the mailboxes; Catz's bassplayer had used his stage name for mail: I.M. Dedd. Apartment Fourteen. Cole kicked through the wine bottles and soggy toilet paper that littered the beaten-up lobby. He went to the antique wrought-iron elevator, which was at least eighty years old, and stepped inside, closing the gate after him. He ignored the sign that said OUT OF

ORDER. And the long-unused elevator began to jerkily rise, its gears and pulleys whining with rust. He stepped out at the second floor, and smiled vaguely at the shoppingbag lady who stood there clasping a sack overflowing with odds and ends, gaping at him. "That goddamnit thingitbob ain't worked for ten goddamnit years," she said, her rheumy eyes on him as if he were a man-sized cockroach.

"Still doesn't work," Cole said, pushing past her. "Don't try to use it." Thinking, *Hell! I've attracted attention to myself.*

The hall stank of urine, mold, and mice. The rug might once have been umber; now it was the color and texture of an oft-trod path worn into clay.

He found Fourteen. The door was unlocked; he pocketed the key and went in.

It was a studio apartment: bedroom, bathroom, kitchenette. There was a First Tongue poster peeling off the flaky green wall like a great loose Band-Aid. Not much else. A cardboard box of wrinkly dirty clothes, a frayed guitar cord, empty beer cans, a lumpy blue-black couch with bricks instead of legs. In the bedroom where the floor sagged alarmingly was a bare mattress full of cigarette holes, a government-ish hypo, and a television set . . . An old TV set from the era without newsboxes or cyberlinks. No card slot on the side. Someone (Catz?) had left the TV on.

The sound was turned off. But the governor declaimed with soundless verve to a news conference, rocking back and forth emphatically behind the podium's many microphones. Cole turned up the sound and sat on the mattress, his elbows propped on knees and chin in palms. He listened abstractedly, waiting for City to make an appearance. The governor was saying:

". . . I think it's very premature, at this time, to say 'the cities are dying' . . . although it's certainly true that the cities are changing, and changing in an extreme sort of way." The governor was a young politician, his colorless hair swept back, his triple-string tie nattily gold against his brown vest. "We can expect to see an upcurve, ah, in the present trend and, as you've noticed"—here he smiled at the reporter who'd asked him the question—"the demographic trend is for redistribution of population away from what we usually call 'core areas.' People are spreading out. AT&T, with its usual recognition of the, uh"—here he cleared his throat while glancing at his notes—"the changes brought about by progress, is opening a composite office that is ninety separate units throughout the suburbs, each unit *in the home* of one of forty-five executives and forty-five assistants, each with a fiberoptic terminal.

"There is simply no office work which cannot be done through a technerlink terminal. And—it can be done faster, since it eliminates the usual tramping about in an office building and the need for handling paper. It saves public energy in the long run, since it eliminates the need for commuting. The benefits are too numerous to list."

He glanced at his notes. "But what are the implications of this? Since all office work, financial and data processing, can be done through technerlink terminals, in coordination with ITF, and since these terminals could be—to pick an extreme example—on the other side of the planet and *still* function well with local units, there is no reason for a business utilizing this, ah, *machinery* to concentrate its personnel in the city. . . . Warehousing, food distribution, freighting—all are becoming increasingly automated. . . . Visionaries foresee for some time, oh, in the next century, a nation of electronically interlinked villages, neat and uncrowded, clean and more livable, eliminating the conditions that create squalor. . . . Those presently living by doing simple physical labor would find equivalent work in the solar panel fields and hydroponic ranches. The system that crowds people into cities gives the impression we're *over*crowded. Actually most of the available livable space in the U.S. is not being used; were people spread out—"

"City," Cole said, swallowing. It had been sudden.

City was there, the governor was gone. City was bigger than Cole had ever seen him on a TV screen, filling it with his unflinching features. His opaqued eyes inscrutable. "You *see?*" City asked. *"Do you see?"*

Cole shook his head.

"You heard what he said," City insisted. "The technerlink people are in with the ITF people and they've got the sonuvabitch in their pockets. The governor—they *own* him." City's voice trembled in earnest rage. "Wasn't it *obvious?*"

"Yes . . ." Cole said, thinking ahead. "Now that you mention it, it *did* seem he was giving the decentralization thing a hard-sell. And naturally technerlink and ITF would have a monopoly, if it came to pass, an' everyone'd be dependent on 'em." Cole spoke in a thoughtless monotone, thinking: *City's complete and unbreakable and cool-but-human and perfect as a movie hero. How can Catz doubt him?*

But Cole's attention returned to City's words with a start as City said: "It wants to kill us."

Cole drew back slightly. "Uh—Who? Who wants to kill who?"

City nodded minutely. "The links. The computer. That cancer in my breast. The thing has to be destroyed—the ITF, the technerlink. They want to spread everyone out over the country, evenly. Regular as hexagons in a beehive."

"The city has its own regularity," Cole said distantly.

"The city's regularity arises from the walls created by competition, and it's the competition of free enterprise. This is a place of metal flexing—*that* will be quiet, efficient, and blasé. With ITF-technerlink *there'll be no need for cities.* No need for *us.* And the Mob wants that moronic uniformity—makes it easier to take us over, catch us unawares. Organized crime, once it's got legal fronts, thrives under the cover of orderliness—"

"I—suppose so," Cole said uncertainly.

"You don't *believe?*" City's face expanded in the screen till there was little left but his shades, brows, and bridge of nose.

Shaken, Cole leaned back on his elbows. "Sure. I believe you—but I'm just not sure this village stuff will, um, really make it easier for the mobsters. Decentralization'll mean they have to spread their boys awfully thin. I got a feeling technerlink might be *in competition* with ITF, and—"

City said: "Are you going to betray me again?"

Cole shivered at the accusation, and averted his eyes. "Hey, I didn't mean—"

"With that woman. You left. Went to another city. I might have needed your help. You listened to her. What about *us?*"

And then Cole felt the beautifully verminous, sweetly squalid, supple but hard-edged *presence* of the city. The blueprints behind his eyelids, the skeins of power and the loci of populace, all of it glowing in the mental dark. And inwardly glowing with the unutterably profound sense of sheer belonging, of unquestionable identity, Cole said: "We'll fight them."

It had to be a bomb. There were some places City could barely reach, inside himself, as a man cannot control the workings of every one of his inner organs; City could open the doors to the computer, but he could not destroy it. Not as he could rend a street or topple a lamppost. But Cole was City's hands.

City had provided the bomb. Cole had retrieved it from a bus-station locker. It was the size and shape of a box of chocolates, but wrapped in brown paper. It fit neatly under his arm. On one corner was a black knob, sticking out through a neat cut in the paper, and on that knob was a white dash. When the knob was turned so the white dash paralleled a black X marked on the paper, the bomb would be set to detonate in one minute.

It was a small but powerful bomb, City assured him.

Cole wondered only briefly who—what human tool— had assembled it, and who had left it for him to pick up.

Now Cole stood outside a squat building of black imitation-granite, the control rooms for the ITF Data Distribution Center. In loyalty to City (in an effort to vilify ITF and squelch his own doubts), Cole pictured the great computer underground as a gigantic mechanical black widow spider squatting amidst terminal linkage lines that were its webbing. . . .

He imagined he felt the huge computer humming through the concrete under his feet. He stood on the sidewalk a few feet from the south side of the almost featureless building, looking about him. He wore a black leather short-jacket, shiny jeans, and sneakers. No mask—they knew who he was. He stood in the darkness below a dead streetlight post, waiting.

The sidewalk split open, the city offering itself to him. The concrete of the sidewalk had slit itself with a brisk but brief *crack!* and now the gap widened, crumbles of cement slipping in the dark opening to make ticking sounds on some unknown surface below. The crack widened, a lower level split, a yellow beam of light angling instantly upward. Cole tucked the bomb into his coat, beside the gun (the gun he'd sworn he'd never again touch). And, glancing around the empty street—it was two A.M.—he got onto his hands and knees, lowered himself into the crevice, and dropped into yellow light and forbidden ground. He landed on his feet, glancing around while fumbling for his gun. But there was no one there. He looked upward, startled by a grinding noise from overhead. The gap in the ceiling closed. He started down the hallway, toward the granite building and the underground computer center.

The hall was scarily wide and bright; he felt exposed. But no one was about.

He padded along, instinctively crouching, though crouching didn't make him quieter or less conspicuous. He came to a cross-hall, looked cautiously around both corners, finding empty corridors.

Yellow tubelights and tile floors to the left, yellow tubelights and tile to the right. Which way? As if in answer, a light to the left began to blink on and off—*thank you, City.* He went left, tugging his gun loose so it swung easily in his palm.

He could feel the city vibrating all around him, its resonations encapsulated and intensified by the subterranean passage. "I'm under *his* skin," he said to himself. And he was drunk with this vast intimacy. So he didn't ask himself: *What the hell am I doing here?* Not just then.

Another fork. A yellow light blinked to the right. A sign on the wall said ITFCC; below, a red-painted arrow pointed right. He went that way. And took three steps. And stopped, hand tightening on the gun.

The autosecur rolled directly for him, leaning ahead slightly as it came, its segmented arms swinging almost lazily. "City?" Cole said. The thing continued to roll toward him. *"City?"*

It skirted him politely and went its way to his rear. He exhaled sharply. "Thanks."

At the end of the hall: a studded metal door set impassably in the wall. The door was inset with a wire mesh bulletproofed glass window. He sauntered up to the window, looked through, and cursed himself for overconfidence. A guard wearing what looked like a grey baseball cap was unholstering his gun. The man was staring from the other side of the door.

The door began to roll back, sliding into the wall. As the window sleighted past, Cole saw surprise on the guard's face. City had made the door open, and that puzzled the man, confused him. City would stop the guard's gun from working.

And Cole was expected to shoot this stranger down on the spot. . . . Cole hesitated, agonizing.

The door slid wholly into the wall. The guard was looking at his gun with redoubled amazement: It wouldn't work. Beyond the man a long hall of metal and lights: the computer.

There was a moment of sheer quiet as the two men faced each other with uncertainty. The hall vibrated, but there was no real *hum.* The computers were eerily silent. Endless banks of chromium—quiet, cold, and confident. Silence is chromium.

The man leapt, and Cole raised the gun. But he held his fire; the guard hadn't jumped at him, but to one side, probably hitting an alarm. An alarm that wouldn't work. And, when it didn't, the guard said: "Shit goddamnit!" But he no longer seemed surprised.

"*My* gun works," Cole said, leveling his pistol at the man's chest.

The guard backed off, staring at the gun and breathing heavily. Now Cole had time to note that the man was young and gangly, tanned, longish hair, probably a surfer in his spare time. He looked strong. His blue eyes narrowing to slits, the man asked: "What—what's the deal? What you gonna do?"

Cole bit his lips. He felt City invisibly at his elbow urging

Kill him kill him kill him kill him kill him . . .

"No," Cole said.

"What?" the man said, startled. His mouth shook.

"Nothing. How many more guards?"

"Six. Most of them upstairs, on break."

Six! City had timed well. "Lie down flat," Cole commanded.

The man slowly obeyed. *Someone's sure to get killed when the bomb goes off,* Cole thought as he moved past the guard and bent to lean the package against a chromium panel. He hesitated, his left hand trembling over the dial.

He hesitated. . . . And something hit him from behind: He'd been over-confident again. He was pitched face down, the guard atop him. He felt his gun hand's fingers compressed by the other man's hand, the stringy bulk, the angry weight against his back. The guard struggled to keep Cole flat, trying to wrest the gun away. Convulsively, Cole squeezed the trigger twice. The gunshots startled the guard, the man's grip loosened, and Cole used the opportunity to twist away. Still holding the gun, Cole jumped to his feet. He turned, ran through the door, sprinted down the hall, hearing shouts from behind him. Other guards had been attracted by the shots; City would close the steel door on them—that would hold some of them. Gasping, tasting iron, his lungs burning, Cole pounded down the hallway, skidding around corners, hating the echo of his running footsteps.

In the distance, above, sirens bayed.

Cole turned left, dashed down a hall, turned right. He wasn't sure where he was going now. A door flew open for him. He flung himself through and up a flight of concrete steps. He found himself in a furnace room just beneath the street. He threaded pipes and conduits, found a metal ladder, climbed clumsily, the gun in his way, reached up with his left hand to wrestle with the wheel of a hatchway. The hatchway turned and opened back for him too easily: City's assistance. He climbed through into night-dark, gratefully sucking in the cool aboveground air. He was in a loading alley behind the imitation-granite building. Lights flashed down the street, sirens passing with the wails of flying ghosts; shouts from around the corner. A pair of headlights swung ominously onto the alleyway, the vehicle filling the narrow passage, charging at him. Panicked, swearing, he looked for sanctuary. His search was futile. The car, its lines obscured by brilliant headlights, drove at him. He flattened against the wall as it pulled up a foot short of him. Its lights went out. It was just an empty cab with one door open. "Oh, thank God," Cole breathed, walking through a hot fog of exhaustion to the driver's side. Best he sit in the driver's seat so no one noticed a driverless cab. The door slammed shut, the gears changed, the lights came on, the wheel adjusting itself as the cab backed swiftly out of the alley and into the street.

They swept to the right. *Too quickly*. Cole thought. *He'll attract attention with his hurry*. Two police cars were on his tail almost immediately. The cab picked up speed, ran a red light (both Cole and City *knowing* that no one was coming crossways through the intersection) and sped onward down the nearly empty avenue. Lights cometed by, pools of shadow, light/dark/light/dark, yin yang yin yang, dark/light; and in the mirror, like red demonic eyes, the whirling gumballs of two patrol cars screaming after, side by side. City's voice from the radio: "You didn't kill him and you didn't set the bomb."

"I *told* you I'm not a fucking secret agent," Cole said, smarting under the implication of betrayal.

The police cars were closing. Another joined the chase from a side street. Soon they'd block him off up ahead.

City intervened. The police cars behind slowed, almost stopped, began to weave around and around in absurd figure-eights, one after another, around and around and around. Watching in the mirror, Cole laughed. How would they explain in their reports? " 'The cars just felt like dancing, sir,' " Cole mimicked.

Then the cab pulled up short; Cole rocked forward, grabbed the steering wheel, barely escaping a nasty crack on the head. Just ahead, two police cars blocking the street blared through their PA's, "STAY WHERE YOU ARE—"

And replacing the gruff amplified voice, music came out of their PA's as their cars began to drive in figure-eights, nose to tail. Disco blared from their speakers, a tune that had been a hit a year before:

Come on baby let's go round and round
Come on baby all over town
Come on baby round and round . . .

Laughing, Cole let the cab turn the corner. Driving at a more leisurely pace, the cab carried him to the apartment in the Tenderloin district.

Cole's laughter contained a touch of hysteria.

SEV-uhn!

COLE SAT IN A DARK PLACE at the top of the city, he sat amidst refuse, gazing at a night carpet of hard city lights spread out below the broad picture window. To his right: a TV set flickered soundlessly; he kept it on all the time. To his left: a half-empty quart bottle of beer and a half-smoked cigar whose ashen ember had long since given its heat to the world. On his lap: the pistol.

City had moved him to the empty penthouse suite in the Rackham Arms, to hide him more effectively from the police and the vigs—someone was sure to search every place connected with Catz Wailen. The penthouse's usual leaser was out of town for the summer; no one had questioned Cole's coming and going since the owner frequently lent the place to friends. The suite was well-stocked with food and drink, its freezer overflowing with meat, its cupboards crowded with canned goods. Cole had immediately disliked the stranger whose home this was, seeing the lavish furnishings and professionally decorated interiors. Cole had no respect for a man who hadn't the imagination to decorate his own home. Now the room was decorated with empty cans and wrappers and bottles and dishes piled to either side of the luxurious furniture.

After providing the suite, City's *presence* had vanished. Cole was alone. There was a sense of the urban overmind, like background crackle of static on a radio, but no real definition. Cole had waited for three days, not stirring from the suite. Waiting for word from City. At intervals he glanced at the television, expecting to see City's staunch features on its screen. But it was Saturday, and still no word from him. The events of the past week were dreamlike in Cole's memory, and he began to doubt the reality of the world outside the glass—the glass that formed an entire wall of the suite. He slept during the day, arose at night to wait.

"I get up to wait," Cole said to himself again. "Stupid. Stupid." He sat cross-legged on the rug, close beside the glass wall; the room was dark aside from the plasmic blue flicker of the TV screen. Cole had adjusted it to black and white—the colors distracted him, made him impatient to go into the world. He existed in a twilight of waiting.

His thoughts returned with annoying frequency to Catz.

He'd called the number she'd given him in Chicago. She was never at home. Once a sleepy male voice had answered and said, "Huh whuh? Oh, she's playin' a gig somewhere. Whoozis?"

There was jealousy in the man's tone, which meant Cole had reason to be jealous.

Cole glanced at the television. Jerome Jeremy, the hermaphrodite talkshow host, was stroking a voguer starlet with one hand and his own breasts with the other. Cole yawned. "Maybe," Cole said to the city lights below, "City's punishing me again. Because I didn't shoot the guy when he told me to and that made it impossible to plant the bomb properly. Maybe he's making me agonize over it on purpose. Maybe he's abandoning me. . . . But then why set me up here?"

"Why indeed?" came City's voice from the TV.

Cole looked. City's face filled the screen. A hallucination out of sensory deprivation? Cole bit a finger and the pain felt real.

If anything is unquestionably real, it's pain.

So City was there, and Cole slumped, suddenly limp, realizing he'd been holding himself tense with expectancy for the waking hours of three days.

Cole got unsteadily to his feet, pounding his legs with his palms to restore circulation. He approached the TV and stood over it for a moment, looking with a mixture of reverence and resentment at the city's face, and then squatted beside the console; it wouldn't do for him to stand looking down on City. *I'm his,* Cole thought. *Catz was right.*

"There's a man at the *Chronicle*. He's a feature writer, does some investigative journalism," City said. "His name's Barnes. Rudolph Barnes."

Cole hung on City's every syllable hungrily, seeking some inflection, some tone of approval—or disapproval. City's voice was cold, but no colder than usual. Cole could be sure of nothing.

City went on, "Barnes knows about Rufe Roscoe and the vigs and even a bit about you. He knows they're looking for you. He knows about the Mafia-ITF links—though that's scarcely a secret anymore. But he's planning to do a major exposé for a national wire service. I want you to go to him, call him and have him meet you somewhere. Be careful, since it will have to be in the daytime tomorrow—he's leaving town tomorrow afternoon. He's in Santa Cruz now, or I could get you to him. He'll be back in San Francisco tomorrow morning, out tomorrow afternoon. You'll only have a few hours. Find him, tell him about Rufe Roscoe's tapes and everything else you know—except about me. That would be a hard thing to convince him of, and I don't want to manifest to him—he lacks the rapport. He's not a citizen of San Francisco—"

Cole thought he detected contempt in City's tone.

"—he's a New Yorker, and loyal to it. But find him—he'll help. Call the *Chronicle* at nine A.M. tomorrow. Get some rest."

"Cit—"

But he was gone.

He was gone; but he'd come, he'd spoken. Stuart Cole wept with relief.

Even on the low-resolution screen of the vidphone Cole could see that Barnes was a florid-faced man, as gaunt as he was ruddy, with almost no chin and a squat nose. But his eyes were intense and penetrating, and beneath the thin-haired, fretful middle-aged exterior, talent vibrated. He was the man for the job.

"Yes? Well?" asked Barnes in a gravelly voice.

Cole took a deep breath and burst out with, "I'm Cole. Stuart Cole. I know what you know about ITF and Rufe Roscoe, and I know more than that."

"Look, pal, it's Sunday," said Barnes with exaggerated weariness. "I try to make it a practice to take Sunday off. I'm just here for a quick conference and then I'm on the plane—"

"Okay, cut the bullshit," Cole said. "I don't have time." It was obvious to him that Barnes was giving him the brush-off just to test his reaction, to see whether Cole was a crank or a ringer. "I'm who I say I am and I'm not going to discourage easily."

Cole shifted self-consciously as, through the monitor, Barnes examined him with open appraisal. Cole wore his hair in a conservative cut; he'd found a very conventional business suit in the suite's closets, and he wore blue-lensed glasses—he'd have blended with the human wallpaper anywhere. Still, he was nervous. He was in a public booth in Chinatown, and policemen passed on their beats at regular intervals. A cop who'd just examined a bulletin photo of him could recognize him at any instant.

"You look like the guy," Barnes said.

Cole was startled. "You've seen a picture of me?"

"Sure, we get all the police bulletins. There's an all-points out for you, pal. I credit you, anyway. You gimme the data-flow you claim and your debit will be backed up unblemished to Fort Knox, at least as far as I'm concerned."

"There's a restaurant," Cole said, "on Broadway, called Luigi's."

Barnes nodded. "How soon?"

"As soon as possible. I'll be watching the place from nearby, and if it looks clear I'll come in when I see you. Don't carry anything conspicuous."

"Okay. But look, don't you think I should—"

"Call the police?"

"No." Barnes grinned. "No, I was gonna say I should bring something that'll back up my story later. A camcorder?"

"Nope. That'll draw eyes to us. I'll tell you when you get there where you can get proof." Cole hit the severance switch and left the blank screen to step into vivid sunlight, blinking. He had grown used to night life; the sun burned his eyes and he blinked away tears. He yawned. He hadn't had enough sleep. He set off up the hill, trying to look like a businessman strolling to a Chinese restaurant.

He toiled uphill through a heavy Sunday noontime crowd, lost in a lava-slow stream of tourists. A parade of sleeveless shirts and sunglasses on the left; the riotously

honking, thrumming cars to his right. The hot air smelled
like sweat, aftershave, various perfumes and deodorants,
fish, and strangely-spiced meats from the Chinese groceries. Sidewalk vendors sold souvenirs and ice cream, caw-
ing over the rising and falling streetsong of a summer day
in Chinatown: "Nice cool ice cream!"

Sweating, overburdened by the full suit, he reached
Broadway and gratefully stood in the shade of an awning
across from Luigi's. He stood with his back to a deli, peering with spurious indifference through the curtain of people drawing back and forth over the walk. He could see the
front door of Luigi's, but the window was opaqued white by
the sun coming from behind him. Barnes wouldn't be in
there already.

Feeling conspicuous now that he was detached from the
main flow of the street, Cole stood rubbing his hands
against the hips of his pants: He was nervous and afraid,
and recognizing this he became more nervous and afraid
out of fear that he was making himself an object of suspicion. Tension mounted in him and he had to restrain himself several times from looking over his shoulder.

A police car trolled the street slowly. Cole's hands balled
into tight fists. He stared straight ahead. The car passed,
but Cole's nervousness only increased.

To distract himself, he thought about Catz. It was near
here that they'd sat in the coffee shop, each wondering
about the other. He smiled faintly remembering the following night. He wasn't so old.

He's using you, she had said.

Cole no longer wanted to think about her.

For no particular reason—no conscious reason—Cole
found himself watching two men who stood across the
street on the corner adjacent to Luigi's. One wore a flowery
red and blue shirt and a camera on a strap about his neck.

He wore swimming trunks and sandals. He was a well-built man, and young, and it seemed strange to Cole that he would dress so much like a middle-aged tourist. Beside him, a tall man in dark glasses, slitted trousers, and a jacket that was, like Cole's, too hot for the weather. There was something odd about the way he stood. Cole stared. He seemed to be leaning to his left, his right side to Cole—and he was leaning over far enough that he should have fallen. Cole watched, keeping his face turned straight ahead, the direction of his gaze hidden by his blue-tinted glasses. The man turned right slightly to glance toward Cole. His eyes flickered over Cole and it seemed, just then, that he looked away rather too quickly. Cole could see now that the man was leaning on a cane. He was a rather young man to have a cane, Cole reflected. And a third man joined them.

The third man—wearing a trim blue business suit and dark glasses—stepped up familiarly beside the other two, but said nothing. Not even hello, unless he did it without moving his lips. And it seemed to Cole that all three glanced his way, by turns.

Cole was breathing heavily, and he felt sweat roll over his Adam's apple and down his collar. *Who are these guys?*

Cole had the impression he'd seen the man with the cane before: it wasn't really the man's face, it was his size, the set of his shoulders the angle of his chin. Like something blurrily recollected from a dream. Where had he seen him?

The cane. His left leg damaged. The man held the cane without the ease of familiarity. He shifted his grip frequently, unused to it. The left leg—one of the vigs at the house in Berkeley, where Catz had been held, had been shot in the left leg. The only one who had survived. The one who would recognize Cole.

Cole turned to dash for a cab turning onto Sutter.

A woman pushing a fat baby in a stroller bulled blindly between Cole and the cab; he nearly fell over her, apologized, sidestepped, and the cab was gone. A tap on his shoulder from behind; fumbling in his coat for the pistol, Cole whirled, expecting to be struck down. Barnes grinned back at him. "Nervous, aren't you?" Barnes said.

Cole looked toward Luigi's. The three vigs were gone from the corner; Cole saw them strolling with false complacency across the crosswalk.

"I got a cab waiting over here," Barnes said. "I thought we might—" Barnes pointed toward a yellow cab on Broadway.

Cole sprinted toward the cab.

Cole heard a shout from behind. "Hey!" And it wasn't Barnes's voice. He grabbed at the back door of the cab, jerked it open, and heard the driver say, "Hey I gotta fare awready—"

"It's all right, we're going together," said Barnes, piling into the car after Cole.

"Please go *now!*" Cole said with widening eyes, watching a policeman running at them from behind. He prayed that the driver wouldn't see the cop waving for them to stop. The cab swung into the street, shot into a gap in the unceasing traffic, and drove through a yellow light and down Broadway. "Head for, uh, Coit Tower," Cole said, choosing a destination at random. The driver nodded.

"I gather we weren't alone back there," Barnes said.

Cole nodded. "Maybe we're still not. They'll follow."

Barnes exhaled a sigh. "Boy, I hope you're not a nut."

"I *am* a nut," Cole said casually. "But I'm going to tell you the truth anyway."

"But—how did those guys know where to find us?"

Cole frowned. "Actually, I was thinking of asking you that."

Barnes raised his eyebrows. "Go on."

"Well—ITF is everywhere, almost literally. With us in this cab—" He pointed at the cab's ITF terminal. "And, uh, how do you figure you could wander around asking questions, dis*turbing* questions about them, and not attract attention?"

"But how would they know where we . . . ?" Barnes stared at Cole, his chinless jaw dropping. "My vidphone. It's probably tapped."

Cole nodded. "Probably for a long time."

They were climbing hills now, winding in and out of mansions, smog-deadened foliage, up toward the Coit parkgrounds.

There was another cab trailing behind, on the sunwhitened street. Cole watched it over his shoulder for a while. Three silhouettes in it besides the driver. "Perhaps," he said, facing front again, "I'd better tell you now. . . . First thing is, Rufe Roscoe has videotaped all the major meetings with his associates."

Barnes rubbed his lined forehead. "That's not too bright of him."

"I know. It seems that way. But there may be a method in it. Anyway, he keeps these tapes in a vault, and if someone could get a court order for access—it'd have to be from the state prosecutor—then they could get the whole organization by the throat. . . ."

Cole paused, noticing the cabdriver watching them in the mirror. The black driver's round face and hard, deep-sunk eyes conveyed the rawest sort of suspicion. "What the hell's going on with you two?" the man said rapidly, his eyes darting from the mirror to the road and back to the mirror.

"Mind your own business," Cole snapped.

The cabdriver shook his head. "Hey, you guys got the fare or what? You talking pretty damn crazy. Last week two guys beat the shit outta me and made me give 'em my goddamn watch I had for twelve year—"

"Look, it ain't likely to happen the same way twice, man," Cole said wearily.

The cabdriver pulled up. Cole glanced over his shoulder. The other cab stopped also.

"Pay the fare right now. Somethin'. I got a feelin' . . . I always know when somebody's card's run out. I got a feelin' for it," the driver said testily.

Barnes snorted and drew his card from the front pocket of his badly filled-out golf shirt. He pressed his thumb to the temporary print pad on the carrier side, left a transient imprint, and handed the card to the pudgy driver. The man slotted the card into the terminal and waited. The tiny screen said: ACCOUNT DISSOLVED. Cole and Barnes stared in amazement.

"But I've got two thousand credit in that account!" Barnes shouted. "I bought breakfast just this morning—"

Cole shook his head resignedly. "You're marked. They saw you dealing with me. They hate me."

"Look here, buddy," the cabdriver began angrily—he stopped, staring past his passengers out the back window. "Who the hell them sluttin' dudes? Hey, that bastard's gotta *gun!*"

Barnes dove down to the car's floor. Cole's hand went to his own gun. He drew it and stared at it and wondered if he could use it again. He looked up and around desperately. It was a prosaic tree-lined street: tall brick apartment buildings, some of them ivyfaced, stood crowded to either side. There was a man looking at them from one window; he closed the curtain when his eyes met Cole's. Cole looked in the rear view mirror. The three men were perhaps thirty feet behind the car, two of them beginning to trot; the man they left behind came stumping along with his cane. All three carried guns.

Knowing he couldn't bring himself to use the gun again, Cole pointed it at the sweating, ogling cabdriver and shouted, "Get out and run!"

The man obeyed, shouting, "Fuck the whole buncha you crazy low-credit mothers!" over his shoulder. Cole climbed over the front seat, tossed the gun on the seat beside him, and shifted into drive. He swung the car in a jerking U-turn, gritting his teeth against the wrenching inertia, and drove at the three men who stood braced just ten feet beyond his hood. One of them flung himself aside, another raised what looked like a Luger to fire point-blank at the windshield. Cole closed his eyes against flame and flying glass; something stung his check. He pressed the gas pedal to the floor, keeping his eyes shut. Two thumps against the car, the wheels jarring squishily over something; another gunshot from the side of the car—Cole heard the left rear window shatter, and a whimper from the back seat. He opened his eyes in time to see a police car jamming itself across the road ahead. Cole jerked the wheel blindly to the right; someone leaped out of his way from the sidewalk; there was a teeth-clacking jolt, the front end bouncing upward as the car struck the curb, drove with two right wheels on the sidewalk past the rear end of the patrol car blocking the street, and swerved around the corner. Sirens sounded from several directions. . . .

Sirens are the background music of my life, Cole thought.

The road careened crazily past; the cars in the left lane honked; cars ahead drove to the right and left to avoid the insane cab speeding up from the rear. Cole honked continuously, warning people to get out of the way. Static crackled from the cab radio, a salad of voices. Driving with one hand on the wheel, trusting to luck as he ran stoplights, Cole had an idea. He reached for the cab's radio and, pressing the talk-button, shouted, "City! You can't physical-

ly interfere in daytime, but you can talk to me! Talk to *them!*
Can't you give the cops the wrong directions? Call them off
me! Fake it out! Pretend to be the police dispatcher!"

"Yes . . ." came a familiar icy voice from the confused
melee of the cabdrivers' frequency.

Soon the sirens receded. Wind from the broken window
in his face, broken glass tinkling on the floor, Cole drove to
a BART station. He pulled up, killed the engine, and leaned
back, breathing heavily, shaking, letting the adrenaline run
its course. A dizziness swept over him, and passed. He
remembered Barnes. He laughed unevenly. "Hey—hey,
Barnes—oh Jeez, boy was I scared. . . . Some pretty damn
good driving, though, huh? Jeez, you just don't know what
you're capable of till you—"

He stopped, remembering the gunshot that had taken
out the side window. And the whimper from the back seat.
Cole didn't turn around. He just couldn't bring himself to
look. "Barnes?" He called, his voice breaking. "Oh god, I'm
sorry. I'm sorry, Barnes."

Finally he had to look. Barnes might need a hospital.

Cole turned around.

Most of Barnes's head was gone.

What frightened Cole most was that the sight of violent
death no longer sickened him.

He abandoned the cab and walked, bleary and exhausted, to the train station.

Cole let the phone on the other end ring, though it had
rung at least thirty times.

A click and a sleepy voice: "Yeah?"

Cole's heart fluttered. "Oh—uh—Catz?"

"Stu?"

"Yeah—why doncha turn on the picture?"

"Oh, my, um, picture tube's out—this phone's all fucked

up."

"Can you see me?"

"No . . ."

Cole wondered if she simply didn't switch on her picture because she didn't want him to see the man in bed beside her.

"Well—what's been going on?" she asked.

Cole laughed humorlessly. "Hardly know where to start. Uh—put on the earplug."

"Okay," she said.

So she *was* with someone. Otherwise she'd have said she didn't need the earplug for privacy. *None of my business.*

Quickly, speaking mechanically, Cole told her what had happened since she'd gone.

There was silence when he'd finished.

Finally he said with grim humor, "Well—how's everything in Chicago?"

When she spoke again he could tell by her voice that she was crying. "Goddamn you, Stu. You're in a madhouse. You're running over people now, and they're getting shot on either side of you, and he's got you setting bombs that you don't know *what* they're gonna do. You're making me *sick,* man. God*damn* you, Stu."

The line hissed to itself in the ensuing pause.

Until Cole said, welling with bitterness, "Catz—I'm scared *stiff.* But I can't leave. I need you. Please—"

"No. Get away from there. Get away from him. He's using you. I don't want you to lose every shred of yourself— look, it's obvious isn't it? I mean, City's scared of the urban concentration getting broken up and spread out over the countryside when technerlink and ITF make stuff obsolete the way it is. *He knows that Cities are obsolete.* He's using the Mob thing as an excuse—but he'd do the same whether or not it's legit. It's the city's *time* to die, Stu, and you've got to get away, man, before you go down with it."

"Look, I can't!" Cole said in a burst of anger. "I need you, but I need—" He stopped. There was an odd sound. . . . The dial tone.

A-A-ate!

THE PENTHOUSE SUITE STANK. It was cluttered with soiled garments, food wrappers, moldy tin cans. Perversely, Cole was pleased by the stench. He was in the mood for negative reinforcement.

Thank God it was night.

He'd had three totally sleepless days; it was Wednesday evening, he had waited impatiently for the day to end; he was no longer comfortable when City was latent. . . .

He paced the curtained glass wall, wringing his hands, every so often peering through the curtain slit—Was the sun quite gone? Yes, yes it was gone.

And Cole began to feel it, a slow oscillation of Presence increasing the frequency of its wavelengths, shivering up his backbone, lighting up his head with the blueprint imagery: the city's neurology superimposing on his own.

"Cole . . . "

Cole went to the TV set and squatted before City's electronically-graven image. "Cole," City said again, as if savoring the name. "Do not go out into the city tonight; you must rest. There is a trip for you tomorrow. Out of town."

"No!" Cole sat up straight, trembling. "No—I get all—worthless . . . when I leave you . . . I think I'd fall apart. I could have done it last week. But things are different now." He knitted his brows, trying to think: How *were* things different?

"We're closer now, true," City said, speaking what Cole had been trying to put into words. "But you've got to go, now that Barnes is dead. I'm sending you to see the State Assistant DA."

"I—look, couldn't we arrange for him to come here somehow? I can *do things* better here. Now. Even in the daylight—I could drive that cab the other day like—like a professional stuntman. Because I'm closer to you now, and the streets and the cars on the streets are more like a part of me. But—out of town—"

Cole gave up. City was inflexible. It was useless to argue. "Do I . . . " Cole began hesitatingly, averting his eyes from the accusing glare on the screen. "Do I, uh, have to go in the daytime?"

"I'm afraid so. That's the best time to catch him. I've made an appointment for you—he has the impression that you're someone other than you are." City almost smiled. "Someone important."

"But—" Cole sat up animatedly, having thought of a valid objection to the trip. "But I *can't* go to the DA's office because I'm wanted by the cops, and with all the mayhem that's happened around me there's sure to be something out to alert the authorities in the rest of the state. Even if you send me under an assumed name, someone's liable to recognize me. Anyway I'll have to let him know who I am in the course of the story to make my evidence believable—you have to be able to prove you are who you are if your story's gonna have substance with the courts."

"I can see you're not keeping up with the news," City said.

Cole wrinkled his nose. "I haven't been watching. I don't want to hear about the . . . "

"The shootings? You needn't have worried. There's been nothing about them. Except the vaguest sort of reference to gang wars. Nothing about you. Few of the police know who you are. Think about it—they're not *all* corrupt. There are guys like Barnes with both the cops and the newspapers. Suppose when you're arrested someone like that questions you and believes enough of your story to go to the federal authorities. Suppose the local FBI become interested. . . . Now ITF doesn't want you to testify one way or the other, or to make any statements. Those cops who *do* know about you have, as of last Sunday, been ordered to shoot you on sight whether you resist or not. They'll excuse it somehow."

"They're whitewashing it? All those people killed?" Cole asked. But he was not surprised.

City just stared back at him.

Finally Cole nodded. "Where and when?"

"Sacramento, State Department of Justice building, room four, three P.M. You leave on the train at noon."

"But—what do I tell him?"

"In the same bus locker you found the bomb, there will be a ticket and a briefcase. In it are transcriptions of one of Roscoe's key videotaped meetings, plus a segment of the tape to help verify it. It should get them started, though it was illegally obtained and can't be used as evidence."

"Obtained how?" Cole asked eagerly. "I want to meet the man who puts the stuff in the lockers, who gets it for you— we could help one another . . . and talk."

"No," said City, his image becoming fainter. "It's not a man. It's an autosecur. Just a cold machine. You would have little in common."

"I'm not so sure," Cole muttered to himself, as City's image vanished from the screen. *Just a cold machine.*

Cole was glad he had a first-class ticket, with a sleeper. Because from the moment he'd passed beyond the subliminal but everpresent reach of City's consciousness, he'd been sick. Even here, in the comforting, rocking dimness of the sleeping niche, Cole was in torment. He rolled from side to side, at one moment feeling claustrophobic, the next rawly exposed. Above all, he felt profoundly alone. His gut was an aching pit.

"Shit," he said aloud, chewing a thumbnail and staring into the twilit corners of the small enclosure, "I'm acting like a child." He tried to find comfort in the regular chirr-click-chirr-click of the electric train's wheels, He longed for a drink. He had to stay alert for the meeting. But it would help if he could numb himself a bit. Just a bit. The void inside him seemed to resonate with every vibration of the train.

Shaking himself angrily, Cole swung from the sleeper, pressing through the curtains over his bottom bunk to get to his feet, swaying in the narrow passage between a score of curtained niches. He made his way toward the lounge car thinking, *Just one or two. Someone will buy me a drink.*

In the noisy, airy walkway between cars Cole encountered a fork-bearded pasty-faced man, short and narrow. The shade-hidden eyes attracted Cole's attention—the mirror sunglasses reminded him of City. The man had short hair, the sides of his head had been bleach-patterned to show Maltese crosses. The man hid something in his army surplus coat as Cole came into the roaring connecting passage. Cole stopped and inspected him. There was a silent exchange between them, and the man relaxed. He took his hand from the breast of his coat, allowing Cole to see the pill bottle he held in pallid fingers. They had never met, but they knew one another: Cole the buyer, the stranger the seller. Street-instinct identified them both to one another instantly, though Cole hadn't bought drugs in years. "Anything for debit?" Cole asked, momentarily forgetting he had no account.

"Trilithiums," the man replied. "Time release tranks. Four each."

Cole considered. He had no account, no credit, nothing.

But he had a gold watch he'd found in a drawer at the suite. It was an expensive digital, calculator and communications linked-in. "All I got's this," Cole said, removing the watch and handing it over.

The man's face registered nothing but his voice was too casual when he said, "Yeah, okay—it might be worth three of 'em." When they both knew it was worth more like three hundred.

Cole shrugged and nodded. The man handed him three trilithiums, which Cole stowed beside his last cigar in its plastic package. Cole found his way back to the drinking fountain, where he downed all three trilithiums. He went to the sleeping niche and lay down, thinking, *How will I get to the Justice Department from the train station? I've got no credit to pay for a cab.*

He lay down, and sank into a delicious ooze of numbness.

As it turned out, the station was a walkable distance from the DA's office, about a mile. Groggily, occasionally bumping into people, Cole wandered through a tranquilizer haze down the street, the briefcase swinging in nearly slack fingers. Squinting repeatedly at street signs, then at the address slip he held in a clammy palm, he slowly made his way to the state capital complex.

Almost sleepwalking he nearly fell over in the waiting room of the assistant district attorney's office. The secretary looked him warily up and down. Cole smiled at her (he hoped it was a smile—his facial muscles weren't working well) and said slurrily, " 'Scuse me, I'm a bit groggy, took some . . . cold pills and I guess I'm a bit sensitive to 'em."

She nodded slowly. "That happens."

"Would you tell Faraday I'm here?"

"I did already, sir. Your name was Stuart Cole and you are a special investigator for the San Francisco City Treasurer's office?"

"Yeah," Cole said, swaying. He didn't remember telling her that, but apparently he had. A realization struck him: The seller had said *time release tranks.* So probably the full effect of the trilithiums was just now hitting him. . . . Cole said "Slutfuck," under his breath. He hoped he could make it through the appointment.

"Perhaps you'd like a seat—" the secretary began. But a voice from a hidden speaker in her desktop said,

"Send him in."

Returning to her databoard, she indicated the door to her right with an upraised thumb.

Cole walked unsteadily past her, trying to orient himself. His legs were a long, long way away. Objects on the edge of his vision seemed to melt together. He pushed through the swinging door and entered Faraday's office. The man behind the broad chrome and synthawood desk was wreathed in fog—Cole blinked, but the fog only thickened. The drug. Cole couldn't see Faraday clearly, but had an impression of an angular, spare man with a neopompadour cut to his thick black hair. "Are you quite all right, Mr.

Cole?" asked Faraday in a rather boyish tone.

"Yes . . . I've got a bad cold . . . cold medicine, you know how it is. Ah—" Cole squinted, trying to distinguish the real Faraday from the other two Faradays in the triple image he was seeing. He blinked hard and concentrated—the three Faradays became one. Cole moved gracelessly forward, thunked the briefcase onto Faraday's desk and, fingers fumbling, managed to open it and extract the papers and videotape; these he placed on the desk under Faraday's nose. "Best we get right to it," Cole said. "I'm not well. All this comprises evidence of—" he searched for words. "Of corruption in the San Francisco police department and the San Francisco branch of ITF—in fact, Rufe Roscoe . . . "

"Actually," Faraday interrupted rather hastily, "I'm aware of the nature of your allegations." He flipped through the transcripts, his eyebrows bobbing from page to page.

It didn't occur to Cole until much later to wonder how Faraday knew the "nature of" Cole's allegations.

"Well," said Faraday, nodding to show that he was impressed by what seemed to Cole a terribly brief glimpse of the materials, "this deserves extensive study. I'll spend the rest of the afternoon on it, and confer with my intelligence boys tonight. Now—I wonder if you'd excuse me; if I'm going to examine these I've got to get right with it; I'm terribly busy these days, I'm afraid. Ah—could you come back tomorrow?"

Cole opened his mouth to reply, then closed it soundlessly. Tomorrow? That would mean he'd have to spend another night and part of a day away from City—an appalling prospect. But he had no choice. He glanced around the office, stalling. Through the drugged haze he made out a large communications screen and beside it a metal cabinet, a machine of some sort.

"Mr. Cole?"

Cole looked up, startled. "Oh—oh yeah, tomorrow, I guess."

He turned suddenly, pivoting on his heel, and almost fell over as he lost himself to the rush of momentum; the combination of lack of sleep and trilithiums had made him ungainly as a string puppet. Steadying himself, he lurched toward the door, pushed through and into the waiting room—and stopped cold. What had he forgotten? The briefcase? He could get that tomorrow. Something else. He'd forgot to arrange an hour for the follow-up appointment.

"Sir?" the secretary's voice from behind him. There was an edge of contempt to her tone. She probably thought he was drunk.

He felt like laughing. He'd sit on her lap to let her smell his breath and reassure her that he wasn't—he caught himself, and shook his head violently. "Go back, arrange an appointment time," he told himself. He turned around carefully, plodded through the quicksand rug back to Faraday's office.

Faraday, standing by the square grey machine (built into the wall, its only features a feed-mouth and a set of dials), didn't look up as he entered. He was feeding something into the machine while speaking to the communications screen to his left. There was a face on the screen watching Faraday, and the face was Rufe Roscoe's. Roscoe was saying, "If you're sure they'll get here in time then don't sweat it, just get the stuff—" he stopped, having seen, on his own screen, somewhere in San Francisco, the TV image of Cole standing behind Faraday. "Damn!"

Cole was staring at Faraday. The assistant district attorney was feeding Cole's transcripts into the machine, a paper shredder. *He keeps one right there in his office,* Cole thought. *Well-prepared fellow.* "You plan to run for office—?"

Cole said aloud.

He didn't see the men who grabbed him from behind, but he struggled against them enough to make one of them hit him in the back of his head. And just as he sank gratefully into unconsciousness he thought, *They're cops, and they're going to kill me.*

NYE-uhn!

THE CELL'S CEMENT WALLS SEEMED TO suck all the warmth from him. Outside, the night was balmy. Here in a Sacramento City jail cell, Cole felt exposed to arctic winds. He shivered, buttoned the top button of his shirt.

When he'd awakened, head throbbing, at dusk, he'd decided they hadn't killed him only because there were too many witnesses about who might be disloyal to ITF. Cole was sure they planned to kill him. Ordinarily an unconscious prisoner would be taken to the jail infirmary. They didn't want a doctor delaying his transfer to San Francisco.

Sitting on the edge of the ratty bunk, Cole nodded glumly. They'd set up the phony escape attempt and the shooting in the morning, during the transferral. It was logical.

He wrapped the rough jail-issue army blanket around his shaking shoulders and closed his eyes, listening to the muted noises of a Sacramento evening coming to him through the high barred window overlooking the street. He let his mind drift, letting the ragged song of the city croon to him, taking comfort in the whirring presence of a city so much like his own, and so distinct. But something was there that he recognized: a sense of invisible organization. He tried to concentrate on that tenuous pattern. . . .

"Over here." A woman's voice, from the metal-cased door.

Cole looked up at the door's barred window. He couldn't see her clearly. *Catz?*

He jumped upright and strode to the door, letting the blanket fall from his shoulders.

But the woman at the door was a stranger. Her hair was flipped to one side, its dyed-red tresses coyly spilling onto her bared left shoulder. The sheer green cling-gown exposed one of her breasts, on which rested a languid white hand tipped in mirror nails; she was full-bodied, her heart-shaped face's original complexion lost in mortis-blue skintint. Her eyes were hidden by wraparound mirrorshades. Cole knew she was a hooker and this knowledge came not from his observation of her clothing and makeup—a voguer might well garishly imitate a hooker's look—but from his awareness of her poise: She was both alluring and defiant. There was something else odd about her: a certain stolid self-awareness, a sense of hidden dimensions. He'd only seen that combination of attributes once before.

"City?" Cole asked tentatively.

She smiled, ever so slightly. Watching the skin of her face move was like observing a slow-motion film of a marble wall buckling in an earthquake. She was hard, hard. "City?" Cole asked, almost convinced it was he.

She shook her head. "No." Her voice was husky, teasing, wise. "I'm not that place. I'm elsewhere."

"How—how'd you get in here?"

"I can come and go as I please in this city. Mostly. There

are a few places here out of reach for me."

"They don't know you're in here?" Cole asked.

"They don't know I'm here. . . . They plan to kill you, Cole."

"I thought so. . . . They didn't bother to read me my rights. No phone call. I guess the only reason the local boys haven't done it is because—"

"—they want the San Francisco heat to take responsibility in case anything goes wrong," she finished for him, nodding.

Cole spat to one side. "How far does Roscoe's influence extend?" he asked.

"Up to Redding, in this state. But the Mob's trying to infiltrate ITF everywhere. They're having mixed success. They'll soon have a great surprise, if the rest of the—the *places* organize themselves properly."

"What do you mean?"

"I mean death. I mean crushing and ripping and sawing of limbs. I mean electrocution and drowning. And all efficiently and selectively. Death for the right people." Cole was sickened by her bland tone. "But we've got to work out a coordination for it. I'm afraid your—your City is not cooperating with the rest of us. He's rather obsessive. He refuses to let go. Your friend warned you—I know, because she talks to Chicago and Chicago talks to me."

"You mean Catz?" Cole asked, gripping the bars, palms damp.

"Yes. She has a good rapport with Chicago."

Things spun through Cole's mind, whirling to a gradual stop as the implications of the woman's seemingly casual remarks came together. And Cole knew: "You're Sacramento."

She nodded.

"And all the big cities have—self-recognizing, um, mentalities? And can manifest?"

" 'Sometimes' is the answer to both questions."

Cole exhaled a long and ragged breath. "Then—you can get me out?"

"Yes—if you'll promise me something."

"Yes."

"Promise me you'll try to convince your City to cooperate with us—in The Sweep. He'll know what you're referring to. . . . If he'd been in closer contact with us he'd have been told that your trip was useless, that Faraday was bought . . . "

"I promise."

And sweet as a baby's kiss, the cell door swung open.

The concrete corridor was empty but for the flutter of a moth. Cole followed her—Sacramento—to a blank wall at the end of the corridor. As if she were removing slices from a soft cake, Sacramento pulled huge blocks from the wall—they seemed to melt to porous pliability under her fingers. Cole tried to help, and only succeeded in bruising his hands. The wall was solid as a solid wall, for him. . . . Methodically she took the barrier apart, stacking the blocks neatly to one side, until she'd made a doorway into an alley.

Then she led him into the night. A driverless cab took them to the train station; the midnight train was just loading.

She kissed him goodbye, her lips against his cheek.

The skin of his cheek burned as if pressed with dry ice.

Catz.

She was waiting for him on the sidewalk outside his hotel. It was four A.M. City's presence was diminishing. The dawn was arcing over the city like the sweep-arm of a radar oscilloscope. It became noticeably lighter out, even as he stood gazing mutely at her.

He shook his head.

He was released from jail, from a trap that should have ended in death. And Catz was here, and he'd been returned to City.

It couldn't last.

So don't waste it, he told himself, and went to her.

They embraced. Cole's weariness, which had been making him stagger moments before, vaporized in the vision of Catz standing in the cleansing illumination of the morning sun, the blue shadows shrinking around her, the mists of evaporating dew rising about her black boots. Now, his arms full with her, he blew out his cheeks with amazement at the variety of feelings welling up in him. ... She seemed strangely small, bony, insubstantial under the leather jacket, contrasting to the monumental stature she had in memory.

He stepped back, held her at arm's length and looked at her. Her goldenbrown eyes were large, the pupils dilated by the shadows through which she'd passed. Her hair was disheveled; she wore no makeup; a few scars on her cheeks stood out grandly in the stark light, making her look wonderfully tragic. She held her lips tightly shut as if to keep them from trembling, so that she shouldn't seem as glad to see him as she really was. She wore a torn pair of ancient straight-legged jeans and a T-shirt under her patched jacket. On the sidewalk beside her was a duffel bag stenciled in white spray-paint: ANARCHY.

She nodded toward the hotel. "Can you get us both in?"

"Yeah ... " He cleared the huskiness from his throat. "Yeah, there's no doorman at this hour; it opens to a key and a voiceprint. City fixed it up for me. But it's only good for a month, till the real renter comes back." He stood gazing at her, his knuckles feeling arthritic with the morning chill. He couldn't bring himself to destroy the mood by moving toward the building.

She did it for him, saying, "Jeez, come *on,*" as she bent to loop her khaki duffel bag over her shoulder. She straightened. "I'm worn out. Rode a goddamn Greyhound. They've gotten *worse* since I was a girl, man. You wouldn't believe it."

Some of the weariness returned to him. He quested through his coat pocket for a full minute before finding the key. They went together to the glass doors. He inserted the key and said, "Tenant." A click. He extracted the key and the door swung open for him. . . .

On the way up in the elevator he told her as best he could through the slogging blur of weariness, of his encounter with Sacramento. She was intrigued by his description of the woman who was Sacramento incarnate. "I'd like to meet her," she said almost reverently. "The apotheosis of whores."

"You seem to have good rapport with Chicago from what she told me. So you could probably tune in Sacramento. I think she'd manifest for you." The elevator rose up floor after floor. Strange to be in an ascending box at four-thirty in the morning. "How did you find out where I was?"

"Chicago's been in and out of contact with City. Apparently San Francisco is a sort of rogue. . . . You said *I* could probably tune in with Sacramento. Like it was out of the question for you to go with me. Because that'd be leaving *here,* as if this hole is some Eden—"

"Hey lay off me, slutter!" Cole snapped. "I haven't slept in days—except when I was knocked out for a few hours, and that wasn't very fucking refreshing. I'm seeing spots and I'm not up for that argument or any other right now."

Catz stared straight ahead at the grey metal door. As if her stare intimidated it, the door opened onto the top floor, and Cole led her down the corridor to the door of the penthouse suite. They went through another electronic opening ritual there, and entered. Catz sucked in her breath. "Ugh . . . Garbage!"

"Sorry. I know it smells. I sort of did it on purpose. It reflected my mood, I guess. . . . I—" He took a deep breath. "I've been miserable without you."

She touched a soft finger gently to his cheek, shaking her head in sad affection.

Throwing aside her duffel bag, she went to the window to open the curtains. "Don't!" Cole yelled. "The sun's up!"

She dropped her hand from the curtain's button and turned on him a look of revulsion.

"It's just, uh—" he stammered. "I haven't had any sleep; my eyes are stinging. I don't want bright light in 'em . . . till I rest."

She chose not to challenge this rationale.

"Come on, then," she said, kicking through the clutter to the bedroom. "Let's get some sleep. My banks are blanked."

"Yeah," he said, following her, relieved at having avoided an argument. "I'm wasted too."

They undressed in the dim bedroom, lay on the naked sheets, basking in one another's company. Feeling that he was sinking through the mattress, Cole listened sleepily to Catz, hugging her near him and seeing just *nothing* in the antiplace behind his eyelids.

". . . So it seemed funny to me," she was saying, "that City told me, through Chicago, where to find you. And didn't try to stop me when I came back. I mean, I think he definitely wanted me out of the way, before . . . It's like he's relented a bit. But maybe it's temporary. Like he's giving us something because he's about to take away much more. . . . Or maybe he knows I can't stay long. I've got to go back to try and get the recording deal together. . . . "

"Speculation," Cole murmured into the pillowcase

dampened beside his parted lips.

"I mean—well how much longer, Stu?" she went on. She paused to yawn. "How much longer can you keep up like this? People weren't meant to live like you've been living. It's no long-term credit, man. You're gonna end up like all those marchin' morons on the street, the gone-schizos that shout at people who aren't there and argue with the lamp-posts and flap their arms all zippy—I mean, it's got to end somewhere. You just can't stay here forever. And—I keep thinkin' of that ghost of yourself you met. I mean—where's it gonna end, Stu?"

He didn't reply, preferring to let her believe he'd gone to sleep.

And a minute later he had.

They slept the day through. When dusk darkened the curtains, they rose and showered, dressed in clean bathrobes. Blue silken bathrobes with some stranger's initials on the breast pocket.

By silent mutual consent they cleaned up the apartment, dumping refuse in great armfuls into the dispose-all. Cole noticed that Catz had unplugged the phone and TV. He said nothing; he could feel City brooding outside the still-curtained windows.

Now that it was night, it was Catz who objected to opening the curtains.

She reached into her duffel bag and produced a cassette player and a small rack of tapes, and turned the volume all the way up.

The tape was a compendium of songs by various artists, popular and obscure, old and new. The music was a sentient presence that brought new living resonance to the walls. The beat, the tireless eternal beat. Just then a late Eighties tune by The Odds, "Sex-Changed Bitch"—

Doesn't matter if it makes you sick
it's all the same, to her tricks
I met her in a leather bar
she took me home to show me her scars . . .

Catz danced while Cole mixed drinks. Cole was too
inhibited to dance sober, A warm gloom deepened in the
living room's corners; the furniture seemed draped in
sheets of shadows. Cole could feel the pull of the city radiating around the hotel: He felt like the axle about which
the City rotated. Still he mixed drinks and watched Catz.
She had let her bathrobe fall open, she danced with manic
intensity, working up a sweat; Cole had the impression she
was trying to savor the final drops of her youth.

The band went on; hard, fast and teasing, the singer
doing a grating imitation of a used-car salesman's patter—

She's better than a real girl
Twice as hot & twice as cruel
She'll do you in the parking lot
For a credit she'll risk getting caught

She's just a sex-changed bitch
Someday she's gonna make me rich
She'll do you coldly but she'll do you best
if you don't mind the hair on her chest

She's just a sex-changed bitch
shit she's just a sex-changed bitch . . .

Cole took Catz a drink and sat down to watch her. In the
dimness her white skin seemed fluorescent blue; looking
strong and thin, her robe swirling around her, she was a
lady vampire newly risen. Cole smiled in approval. She

danced, spilling her drink.

The song ended, another began, and Catz spun to fall on the sofa beside Cole, one hand tilting her scotch and coke back, the other trailing along Cole's neck and shoulders. She straddled the sofa's arm, rocking.

Cole had downed his second scotch when Catz took the glass out of his hand and threw it sharply against the bar, narrowly missing the dim red light, their only illumination. The glass shattered, and Catz laughed; Cole understood that she hadn't done it in anger. He grabbed her glass and threw it against the front door; it failed to break. Catz laughed at him and let herself slip off the arm of the sofa onto his shoulder, so that her weight bore him flat onto the cushions.

He opened his robe, the drinks making him feel misty, and she writhed against him; his upper half was soft, his lower concentrated into hardness, a hardness she enveloped with her lips, while his hands traced the muscles in her back, evoked electricity from her spine. There was a mutual rippling, muscles subtly oscillating from one to another at the same wavelength. She enclosed his axis with a compass, her compressed thighs. And he almost succumbed. But she sat up, letting his rigidity snap back against his round belly, and moved up to straddle him, inching and squirming till both sets of her lips had come into play. The music was a rhythmic keening, a counterpoint thunder, a backbeat thudding, and the clash of sword on buckler was heard in the ring of guitar pick against metal strings.

After a time of ragged breathing and soft exhalations, they rolled away from one another, and she got up to shower.

But it wouldn't be the last time, that night. There was, Cole realized dimly, a desperation in their coupling drive, there was a need to do as much as possible in the time that remained.

The morning, Cole thought. *Something's going to happen in the morning.*

It was nearly midnight when Catz got dressed and went out to take care of band business; midnight was prime working time for the people she was to deal with. Cole fell into a restive sleep.

At twelve-thirty he had a dream. He dreamed his arms were arguing with one another over who should rightfully possess his shoulders. And his legs fought for ownership of his hips. But the hips and shoulders protested shrilly that they owned their own segments of the anatomy and in fact *they* should have jurisdiction over the legs and arms, and not the other way round. While the arms argued heatedly that they should determine the fate of the shoulders and the shoulders ranted their claim over the arms, and the legs and hips fought over territory, the stomach and the groin began to quarrel. The groin claimed that the entire body should be given over to him, since reproduction was surely the prime imperative. The stomach angrily protested that Cole's physical person should become entirely stomach, since any fool knew that eating was universally accepted as Number One priority.

Only the head was silent.

Cole woke, conscious of being alone (except for the city wheeling around the suite, turning around Cole the human axis) at two A.M. He was lying on his back. He blinked. He was covered with sweat, yet he felt very cold. Cold and hollow. He was wide awake. rigidly alert. What had awakened him? A feeling of something crawling onto his right arm. He swallowed and took three deep breaths. He had a violent dislike of rodents. Perhaps a mouse was crawling on his arm. Or worse, a rat. What if it should gnaw him? Trying to move only his left arm, he reached out and switched on the lamp on the floor beside his mattress. He held his breath and turned to look, raising his left hand to fling the thing away.

There was nothing there, except a lamp cord, unplugged. One of two lamps. Odd the cord should be lying on the bed. It lay like a vein across the blanketless wrinkled sheets, stretching to the dead lamp on the glass lamp table beside the bed. *Why am I staring at that cord?* Cole asked himself.

Catz must've tossed it on the bed as she left; perhaps it had been in her way.

But what was it he'd felt moving across his arm? A dream.

He tossed the cord off the bed and lay back, feeling oddly heavy, grateful to recline. It was another forty-five minutes before he found his way back to sleep.

He slipped away, seeming to sink through the mattress to deliquesce into a liquid that raced merrily through pipes beneath City's streets. While overhead, luminous blueprints, the buildings and utilities denuded and made neon-visible, blinked on and off in a machine choreography. . . .

Something woke him at four A.M. A tightness on his right arm: the lamp cord, tight around his biceps, the plug-end digging its copper prongs into his shoulder like the dulled fangs of a snake.

He shouted something mindless and flailed his arm, flinging the cord off. The flesh was marked where it had bound him.

There was a double contusion on the shoulder where the prongs had dug, and the wound tingled with malignant numbing. He raised the arm to better see the wound, but the numbness spread till the arm was suffused with it, the flesh impossibly heavy; he had to let it fall back onto the bed. *It's just gone to sleep,* he told himself.

He tried hard to operate the arm. It wouldn't move.

He heard himself whimpering. He choked it off. He got up, staggered, coughing bile, feeling as if he were trying to walk in a jet that had gone into a dive, the G-force dragging him down. He made the bathroom though his limbs were wobbly, the muscles responding poorly, as if they desired to go somewhere else entirely. He stumbled to the sink, fumbled through Catz's kit with his working hand—the other swung, dead meat at his side—and pried open a bottle of sleeping pills. He took six, without water. He staggered back to bed and turned out the light.

Cord got tangled when I moved in my sleep. A nightmare of some kind, he told himself. *Sickness. Be gone when I wake inna morning.*

He fell into sleep like a boulder off a cliff.

But in spite of the sleeping pills he came awake at six. The sun drove slanted, rouged rays through the spaces between curtains.

Cole tried to sit up. He couldn't move. He looked down at himself.

The cord was wound around his neck. *Two* cords, one around his waist. Cole was able to lift his head on the pillow to see over the edge of the bed to the right; the cord that was slowly tightening on his throat ran over the mattress edge, down the side of the bed, under the glass table—but didn't run into the lamp as he'd thought. It had been torn loose from the lamp. The severed end, meant to feed into the lamp base, was jammed into the wall socket. He felt something probing, gnawing at the base of his skull. It tingled there—but there was no electric shock.

But then, he realized with a hysterically objective reasoning, he could feel very little altogether.

His limbs felt heavy, dead, swollen.

Doubtless he was receiving a powerful electric current that he simply couldn't feel. *Doubtless. No doubt. Probably. Seemingly.* Mocking, tinny words sputtering through his failing brain.

Cole gurgled and blacked out.

When he woke it was nearly noon. But Cole didn't know what time it was. He couldn't look at a clock, because he couldn't move. Things were moving over him. Snaking over him, crawling. Cords, black electrical wire, sliding, tightening sinuously over him. Changing him.

City? A soundless shriek. *City!*

No reply.

And where was Catz? But she'd said she would be gone till the following evening. *Just as well she's not here to see this,* Cole thought. *She'd try to interfere. Useless to fight.*

Cole knew he was dying.

Sometimes madness is not an aberration. Sometimes it's a necessary adjustment. Sometimes it's the only way out.

There are certain terrors that cannot be faced without madness. It's always been that way, and a great many people have said it. It's a truth everyone knows. *There are certain terrors. . . .*

And one of those terrors is creeping paralysis, the kind of paralysis that feels like forever. To be trapped under the weight of a city; to be buried alive; to become a man of stone; to be frozen—thinking, feeling, experiencing the slow shutdown of self.

It felt to Cole as he'd imagined it would feel to be trapped between two closing walls, gradually jellied in the flat jaws of a monster vise.

Cole had wondered if City could make it painless for him. If City *would.*

He wouldn't. The pain was coming, through the numbness like a great hideous semitruck looming suddenly in a thick fog, bearing down on him, full of noise and an unspeakable metallic momentum.

It hurt that much.

There are certain terrors. . . .

Cole couldn't make a sound. But he laughed internally. He wondered, as the pain sang up and down his spinal cord and undulated in raging waves through every nerve—he wondered what had become of Pearl. And Catz. And—

He laughed because he was beyond screaming.

City—

A white roar . . .

Cole stared hard at the ceiling and pretended it was everything.

He was crushed under the weight of a city . . . till death came and took the weight off his shoulders.

It was the sound of Catz's voice that brought him out of it.

He found himself standing by the bed, staring at her. He couldn't remember getting up from the bed. He remembered that he couldn't move, there on the bed, and he'd been trapped and strapped and—altered. And then a kaleidoscope of City's blueprints. and a sucking darkness. And here he was, looking at Catz, who stood at the bedroom door, yawning and rubbing her eyes.

It was eight P.M. The room was dark, the figure on the bed obscured.

Who was on the bed? Cole wondered. "Catz?" he said, his voice echoing strangely. It was a voice and not a voice. He giggled.

There was someone on the bed.

Catz reached out and switched on the overhead light.

Cole blinked. The figure on the bed was transparent. The whole room—Cole looked around wonderingly—was transparent. And Catz too was transparent. Like poor holographs. The walls were made of an oddly static mist through which he could see their wires and beams and the farther room and the hall beyond . . . and beyond that, the mist thickened to conceal the rest. He looked down at his own hand. It was solid, it was real. He was the only corporeal thing remaining in the world, it seemed.

And the figure on the bed was himself. It lay sunken deeply into the bed, as if it weighed a great deal. Which was strange, since it was translucent—seemingly tenuous.

And then everything clicked, and Cole made a hundred realizations one after another, until he staggered and held his head with it all. Here are three of those realizations:

(1) He himself had died. Was dead.

(2) The figure on the bed was his body, transformed and taken.

(3) From his viewpoint—that of his new body (astral body?)—the world was tenuous, was here and yet was not here. It was revealed for the fabric of transient illusion that it was; but from her viewpoint it was Catz who was solid, who was real, and Cole who was dead.

That's three. Add a fourth:

(4) He himself lived. Was alive; in a new body, a new state of being. Only the old Cole was dead.

He was alive, and he could think. But he was no longer sane.

City had killed the old Cole—had taken his body, prepared by the extended rapport, for possession. The body of a man possessed by an entire city—this is what lay on the bed.

Catz was screaming.

She was shaking the shoulder of the erstwhile Cole, trying to pound life into its chest with her hands. Where her knuckles impacted, she bled. Seeing this, she drew back, her quivering fingers spread over her wide-open mouth. Her eyes wide and bleak with new understanding.

The nude body on the bed had turned to stone.

But stone animated by City could be made to flow, to flex and ripple as flesh. The figure on the bed stretched, the bed creaking with its great weight. Its eyes remained closed. It sat up. Its head went back and forth, from side to side on the neck as if it were a radar dish scanning the room. It stood, slowly, and went to look into the mirror on the opposite wall. Its hard, etched features remained grimly set. The face was Cole's, the expression was City's. The once-Cole raised its hands together to cover its eyes, the upper half of its face hidden by cupped palms. It remained thus for ten seconds while Catz stood flattened in horror against the wall; panting, staring. Then it lowered its hands, and where it had had eyes there were now mirrorshades, the frames merged with the flesh around the eyesockets. City turned to look at Catz, filling his mirror eyes with her. Catz's expression—revulsion—was doubly reflected there. "Catz!" Cole said. She glanced toward him, startled. She didn't seem to see him—but she'd heard him. "Can you see me?"

"Stu?" she asked tentatively. She squinted. "I can almost—something's there, but—"

"Catz—" Cole began. Her head perked up. She'd heard him.

"Stu!"

The figure by the mirror—City—turned to look at Cole. Cole could feel its eyes on him. He could feel the City around him, as a swimmer senses something of the whole of the ocean's deeps beyond him though he swims in shallow water near the shore . . . resonations from great, distant depths. The squares of the city ringing with the passage of traffic and human toil, the cries of children—

City turned away from him and the sense of total urban-being receded into the background. City moved toward Catz, was reaching a cold hand for her shoulder. *"This is not your place,"* said the iron lips below unbreathing nose and mirror eyes.

She made a sound, "Auh—auh—op—auh—" and backed away from him, rubbing the bruised place where his fingers had brushed. She turned and walked from the room, and Cole heard her say, "I'm sorry, Stu."

Something warm passed away from Cole, and he ached with his newness.

City turned to him and said, *"Go where you will. Walk the breadth of space and the length of time. But don't interfere with me. It's time for The Sweep. . . . "*

Shimmering, walking through doorways made of shimmer along planes of shimmer, City left Cole alone with the whole world.

TENNN!

THREE OF THE SEVEN MEN in the conference room were thinking solely about supper just then—seven-thirty P.M. on a Thursday. The other four were thinking about supper *and* about plans for the evening (one of them—the attorney— was caught up in a sexual fantasy; with his left hand he nursed the erection under his pants pocket) and, as marginally as possible, they considered the business of the meeting. They were weary of the discussion, and the subject had become increasingly painful. *The saboteurs.* They didn't like thinking about the saboteurs (some maintained it was just one man, but a tired club owner alone could hardly be responsible for the attempted bombing; the killing of several vigilantes; the disruption of the rock concert operation; the propagandistic holos; half a dozen other inexplicable events not excluding the massacre of gunmen *cum* vigilantes slaughtered by an impossible eruption of drainage pipes and streetlamps) because the implications frightened them. It had all been very smooth, till recently. . . . So the discussion had gone from rhetoric flinging to debate to petulant contention to hem-hawing, concluding with a trickle of sighs and shrugs. The problem had no solution without further data: Put it off.

Rufe Roscoe was, naturally, not pleased with the outcome of the meeting. There was a singular lack of resolve, it seemed to him. His council seemed limp and indifferent. *Smug Bastards.* Maybe, he thought, they shouldn't hold their meetings in this air-conditioned room high and safe in an earthquake-proof skyscraper. It was a womb with a view—too comfortable, perhaps. When he'd first started out twenty-eight years ago, the planning had been done in cheap, sweaty, smoke-filled rooms with the clack of pool tables and the mutter of roulette wheels coming from the next room; that vulnerable environment had reminded them constantly that they could be higher, could be safer, and that knowledge had driven them. It was in such a room that he'd first suggested the computer embezzling scheme that had made him his first million.

Here? Pastel walls, Muzak cooing from some hidden speaker, a drift of clouds outside the polarized window . . . the men in the conference room were one and all lulled by this complacent cage, convinced of their defensibility, smug in their shared knowledge that no one could attack them here (and never mind the two in masks who'd come into a room like this on this very same floor and shot the man from back east—new precautions had been taken, very extensive precautions, and it could never happen again). They were secure.

The locked door to the conference room flew from its hinges and slammed into Fred Golagong's narrow Oriental back, breaking it in three places and killing him instantly.

In spite of his panic Rufe Roscoe thought: *Serve the smug bastards right.* . . . As the man framed in the doorway (and though Roscoe had never seen him in person before, the man was no stranger—he was a familiar figure from a certain strange recurring dream) moved like a steam engine to smash the conference table; guns went off from three directions, one from the hall behind, and men screamed shrilly. Only one of these cries was rational, and this was from Rufe Roscoe: "What the fuck happened to all the fancy guards and all the fancy alarms?" Which is the last thing he said in that particular lifetime, inasmuch as the man with the mirror sunglasses and the arms powerful as drawbridges killed him with a single blow seconds later.

There were seven men to kill, but it took only a minute and a half.

The Sweep was begun, and San Francisco was doing his part.

Eight P.M. in Phoenix, Arizona. A warm night.

Phoenix is a city with construction work forever building up the urban scar tissue that men call housing projects. Construction and destruction, men making dedication speeches about the eternal cycle of death and rebirth, building the new in the ashes of the old, the ashes from which, presumably, the phoenix would rise.

And like the head of some ungainly metal bird the robot wrecking machine raised up its derrick, its crane drawing in the ten-ton ball on its cable. Like a bird raising its head on a long neck to gaze about it. It nested in the ruins of a great building, a concavity tumbled with uneven chunks of masonry and splintered timbers.

About the whirring crane the deserted wrecking site, the building three-quarters spooned out, showed the cutaway cells of one of the last nineteenth century edifices remaining in the city. It had been a grand place once, the pride of the town, replete with carved angels upholding the cornices and ornamental roof-spouts. It had been a solid place, built for permanence of good wood and stone, and it would have served well for another century if not for the avarice of a certain land developer. . . . The architect who'd designed the old building had, in 1891, twisted his handlebar mustachios in pride over the finished blueprint. He had not foreseen, nor even conceived this day, the day his solid but elegant brainchild lay in raped wreck about an unfeeling machine, its assassin.

But as if that assassin had developed an understanding of the heritage it had laid waste, as if it were determined to avenge the murder for which it had been the murder weapon, it switched on its camera eyes and its running lights and trundled its countless tons out of the wrecking site and down an uncrowded side street.

It had awakened without the help of its programmer, and without its programmer's direction it followed a purposeful course through the maze of side streets, confusing traffic and triggering five kinds of alarms.

Everyone got out of its way; no one stayed to question the impossible.

It was only six blocks to the wrecker's destination: a new office building, constructed in six hexagonal stacks with transparent vertebrae between each floor linking them with escalators and elevators. It was a place built of polarized plasglass and chromalum strips; it was self-contained in its decorative upsweeping floodlights. On the second floor of this gleaming structure three men and two women argued heatedly.

One of them, Lou Paglione, smote the table repeatedly with the flat of his hand, emphasizing his words, "I don't care"—slap!—"if the man thinks he's the don for the whole western hemisphere"—slap!—"he's still got to do things according"—slap—"to"—slap—"procedure!"—slap! He straightened, thrusting his hands in his tweed trouser pockets, pleased that he had everyone's attention. He was perhaps the least imposing man in the room—narrow-shoul-dered, pot-bellied, baldheaded, thick glasses, overall resem-bling a junior college bookkeeping instructor—but every face turned to him with respectful expectation.

"Now then," said Paglione, scratching an ear, "it may seem to you to be a small thing, but to me it's very large indeed. Mr. Rufe Roscoe makes arrangements to commu-nicate with every city board after the meetings with a data-trans of the minutes; some of us in a near enough time zone he will communicate with directly. Oh yes! Never mind that, God knows, we've got our own schedules to keep to—and then he disregards his own instructions. . . ." Paglione waved toward the blank screen that was also the tabletop separating the five seated directors of Sunset Operations West, the cover organization for the computer infiltration branch of the Phoenix syndicate.

A woman with cynical blue eyes and a drawn patrician face under a cobra-coil blond wig pursed her wire-thin lips and suggested, "Best we remember, Lou, that Rufe Roscoe has *always* done what he promised to. This is the first time . . . and this was an important meeting, too. It's not like him to schluff it. And then the fact that there's no answer at all at his building—well, he would have had an answer-ing service at least; but there's not even that."

Paglione frowned, nodding at the blank blue-grey screen. "You think something's gone wrong." There are var-ious ways to say *gone wrong;* Paglione said it meaning, *He's been attacked.*

"There's been stories about crazy goings-on," said a young man tentatively. "I—uh—didn't cred it. But it doesn't bounce so badly now. . . . I'm beginning—"

He made a strangling sound deep in his throat and stared at the darkened swathe of window behind Paglione. Paglione turned to look. "What? Who?" he said.

The window had been dialed to semiopacity, but anything large enough and close enough was discernible as a silhouette.

"It's just some kind of shadow," the woman said petulantly, turning from the window.

But Paglione continued to stare. The silhouette loomed larger with every second: It was a monstrous shape, a skeletal giant with a great round fist. The young man abruptly got to his feet; he strode to the window and dialed the glass to transparency.

Paglione had not become a local don by ignoring his hunches. So it was that he didn't see the wrecker swinging toward the window; he was already running through the hall to the escalator.

But the young man and the others saw it, and they had time for a scream apiece.

It was too unexpected and too near (and too large) to be recognizable in that instant, though it was outlined sharply against the flashing scales of the city lights; to the four people remaining in the room, it was simply the gargantuan instrument of their deaths. Before there was time to draw breaths for a second round of shrieks, the room exploded; great shards of glass and chromalum, blood and gobbets of flesh, rained on the skyblue synthetic rug of the street-floor office below.

Paglione, just bounding off the down escalator (which was frozen for the night; he'd taken it four steps at a time) onto the tiled carport, tripped and fell as the ground shook and chunks of silicon murder crashed about him. None of the glass struck him squarely; he got to his feet, making a sound something like "Aaak, aughk!" in the hysteria of flight.

The wrecker was taking the building apart with lethal efficiency, its magnetically directed ball slicing purposefully through corner junctures and braces, pulling the structure apart strategically, almost thoughtfully. Microwaves transmitted from the wrecking ball itself, coming into play selectively in the more resistant sections of the building, softened the girders for the blows. Within fifteen minutes the entire multimillion-dollar four-month-old structure had folded in on itself and collapsed like a house of cards. The city resounded with the crash.

One of the many firemen, watching in amazement from the parked trucks nearby, whistled softly to himself. The man next to him smiled in a peculiar sort of dreamy satisfaction. "Like a dream I had the other night," he said. "Funny thing . . ."

"Yeah, I dreamt it too."

The firetruck, part of a shiny crowd of varied emergency vehicles gathered in response to reports of a runaway cyber-wrecker, was parked at an angle outward from the others; its engine was dead, its lights off, there was no driver. But, driverless, the truck started itself and swung into the middle of the street, startling the firemen on its hose-rack. It hurtled toward the figure of a man scuttling down the sidewalk. A small man, his thin hair askew, his balding pate gleaming with sweat. He looked over his shoulder and said, "Aaak, aughk!" as the firetruck ran him down. And then Boss Paglione was dead, and the wrecker stopped wrecking and the truck rolled to a stop and a special part of the collective overmind of Phoenix became dormant again.

Several hundred thousand people, asleep or dreaming awake before their TV sets, grunted to themselves in satisfaction. They could not have told you what it was they were proud of themselves for having done. But the pride was there, and a nest of parasites was dead.

Phoenix had done its part.

*　　*　　*

And in Chicago ... And in Sacramento ... And in Portland, Seattle, Boise ...

... In Manhattan a group of grim-faced men were driving to a meeting in an armored limousine. This armor was of very little use when the car inexplicably took its own course, speeding through the Lincoln Tunnel (which was not in the right direction at all) at eighty miles an hour, its instrumentation refusing to respond to the frightened driver. It was just on the other side of the tunnel, in a broader, less crowded place, that they met another limousine head-on. A witness later described the crash as "spectacular."

The second limo, also careening at high speeds with a will of its own, had contained four very influential men from Boston, on their way to meet the very men with whom they'd collided. The meeting was profoundly consummated.

... In Houston was a tower. It was taller than Seattle's Space Needle, but in fact it wasn't much different; it was taller, sleeker, glassier, more modern—which is to say, built with poorer workmanship. Like the Space Needle, it had a restaurant in its topmost cupola, and the restaurant rotated to take in the impressive Houston skyline and the Gulf of Mexico, all in a forty-five minute sweep. This night the restaurant was not rotating. It was closed. It was quite empty, except for the seven men and two women who sat at one of the tables, drinking and arguing, pointing at a blank terminal that sat beside the sugar dispenser. This cabal of nine was unaware that it was alone: No one had noticed yet that their guards and their single bartender had all departed the place (just as Roscoe and Paglione hadn't known that their own servants had been called away, leaving only the unquestionably guilty); the city had tricked them into leaving.

One of the Houston Nine raised a hand for silence and

called petulantly to the bar, "Jude, f'r Clearance's sake, whatcha got the zipping place turning for? I get seasick when the damn thing rotates!"

The others, surprised, looked up at the grid of glaring city lights and noticed, ah yes, the restaurant was in fact rotating.

There was no reply from Jude.

"Hey!" the woman called, her brows coming together. "Hey . . ." this time softly. "Hey the—slutting fuck!" And this because she'd fallen, trying to stand; the pace of the restaurant's turning had increased suddenly, throwing her off balance. She never got back to her feet. In seconds, the city lights were meteorite trails and then continuous streaks of light; the tower's top revolving faster than its engines alone could possibly have turned it. And faster.

There was a lot of shouting up there, but the tower was too high above the rest of the city for any of the shouting (and then panicky yelping and then shrieking and then whimpering and then nothing) to be heard by the sleeping populace below.

It's amazing what sufficient centripetal force can do to human flesh. It just goes to prove that muscle-and-bone's not as solid as it looks. . . .

. . . And in Miami . . . In Biloxi, Atlanta, Los Angeles, San Diego, Detroit . . .

"Half the nation's scared," Cole said to himself, "and the other half is awed."

"Yeah. There's been a gush of religious conversions," Cole replied. For Cole was not speaking to himself figuratively. He had met himself again, himself disembodied, coming from another time-convergence: they paused at a probability juncture to chat.

Each knew what the other was about to say before it was

said, of course. Still, it was necessary to say it, and to listen. A litany.

One Cole was on his way to witness his own birth. The other was on his way to watch his first encounter with Catz Wailen; he'd just come from watching his own birth (and on his way to that witnessing had encountered himself coming back from it; in this way are the patterns of Oriental rugs conceived). They stood on the sidewalk outside the boarded-up Club Anesthesia. The city around them wavered in and out of translucency, time flows converging and splashing apart, moving people seen as tubes of strobo-scopic event-traceries winding along the streets. The Coles were solid—to one another.

"Just speaking Cole to Cole," said one of them leaning forward, "doesn't the neutrality of our position annoy you . . . us?"

"At times. It's true that I feel very little of this plane on a somatic level. When I pinch myself, that hurts—but when I slam my hand into the ground, it's mush . . . although it's concrete to them. So, uh, that implies that there's some level I—we—can and probably will go to in which we can physically interact with the surroundings in a fuller sense."

"We'll end up there," the other Cole agreed, scratching his nude groin. He frowned. "Neither of us is wearing clothes . . . but I remember meeting myself when I got the warning about the vigilantes in Oakland, and that, uh, *self* had clothes on. . . ."

"Oh, in another relative time sequence you—I—will de-cide to put some on. See, clothing that you wore was close enough to your body that it's been psychically soaked by the, um, characteristic vibrations of what you and I *are*. . . . That's how psychics can pick up on where people like, you know, missing people, are—can find them—by touching a sample of their clothing. . . . Something to do with absorptions of electrons whose spins are characteristic of your own electrical field. . . . Anyway, you can put on clothing you wore in life—the other life—and it'll be taken into our plane."

"I knew that already," said the other Cole. "I don't know *why* I asked you."

They laughed.

They stood in a time corridor whose perspective showed the world around them in an event-pacing of greater frequency, hence the man-shaped tubes winding up and down the streets marking the passage of pedestrians. Were they to step into a time corridor of a less frequent event-cycle, they would see the world as other men saw it, one human step at a time, however hazy, refractory, many-layered.

Nearby them now several stroboscopic man-shaped tubes had intersected, were milling with the effect of several huge ribbons knotting into a flesh-toned bow. . . . "They're grouped like that on streetcorners and in taverns all over the city, arguing about the reasons for all the Mafia dons getting offed," Cole said to Cole. "It'll probably be explained away as a vengeful millionaire killing them all in secret—vigilante-style with unknown technology. . . ."

"I knew you were going to say that."

"I knew you were going to say that."

As one, they laughed. Simultaneously they went their separate ways.

Cole strolled, chuckling to himself, beside his city-possessed body. The City that strode beside him—real in several planes at once—was employing Cole's deserted body as a vehicle; but Cole had difficulty in considering this manifestation of City as a version of himself, as a thing possessing what had been Stu Cole. Partly it was the mirrorshades sunken at the edges into what had been his own skull, partly it was the set of the features, grim as the metal face of an onrushing train engine. City had dressed in a coarse uniform of khaki, and a slouch hat. His trousers were torn by the walls he had tumbled, the bullets he had stopped. Cole was dressed in a suit, though he was barefoot, They were walking together along a poorly lit street in San Rafael; in the dark, things seemed almost solid to Cole.

He reflected that he didn't resent the pirating of his body. It had been inevitable; he'd played into City's hands. And City wasn't responsible, particularly. No more than anyone else in San Francisco. He was simply a physical manifestation of the unconscious frustrations forming and deforming in the collective unconscious.

"I don't understand why they're still banded together, since their employers are dead."

"For safety," City replied. "Which is stupid of them. They're clustering together because they figure whatever killed their bosses will want to kill them. They're right. But it wouldn't be so if they didn't stay together; since they're a unit, a cancerous cluster, I'll have to destroy them. And let them destroy me—"

"Oh? It's necessary, that last part?"

City nodded, barely. "As before. The blood insemination."

Cole said dreamily, "Like when they hit you with the car and your blood ran onto the street and the street was awakened and rose up to avenge you. . . . It's a ritual."

"If you like. It's necessary."

Someone was approaching. A little girl walking a small terrier. The girl and the dog flickered in and out of transparency, their respective inner organs momentarily visible, patterns of bloodflow delineating their bodies. Cole shared their time frame, observed them in one place at a time, step by step. Beside them was someone solid. It was a grown man, naked and weeping. A man who'd been in his thirties when he'd died, Cole guessed. They passed Cole and City on the right; the girl widened her eyes when she saw City, but said nothing; her dog stiffened and strained on the leash, jumping into the gutter to get as far from City as possible. The little girl didn't seem to see Cole or the man beside her. Probably he was her newly-dead father. He was the first inferbodied spirit, besides himself, Cole had seen. But the man merely nodded at Cole and returned his gaze miserably to his daughter. "Twyla," he said plaintively. She didn't hear him, but the dog perked up his ears and yanked free, scampering across the street with the leash rasping on the asphalt, the girl chasing the dog and shouting, her unseen father stumbling after her, sobbing.

Cole felt cold inside. For the first time since his own transition, he was unhappy. And feeling that, he sensed the call of another place. Where?

"You are going to leave me?" City asked. There was a trace of regret in his voice.

"No," Cole said after a moment. "I'll never leave you. Never, as long as you exist. In forty years or so, *their* time, the city will be almost dead. ITF and the other systems will make the Global Village possible. All communities will be small—a few hundred people—and a different sort of collective mind will take shape. And then you won't be here to need me, and I'll go to that other place. I'm freer now, somehow. I'll travel to other cities. I've got to go to Chicago shortly. But I'll always be here in another time frame, and the foremost—relatively speaking—the foremost Cole, evolving concurrent with the timeflow, will always return to you."

Cole had spoken softly, reassuringly. City had listened without expression, walking on implacably through the night. But he'd heard. He and she and they—all who were City knew that there walked among them an invisible friend.

They paused in front of a ranch-style house with flood-lights on the neatly mowed lawn. Two German Shepherds snarled from their tethers near the front porch. "This would be the place," Cole said dryly. "Uh—are you going to merge somehow, here?"

"Yes. This is part of my city. They have a store of plastic explosives in the basement. I'll detonate them. You might come in and enjoy the explosion—it's quite an experience, riding a blast that doesn't hurt you. It's glorious."

"All explosions are glorious," Cole agreed. "City—why aren't you radiating music now?"

"House music? It's not necessary now. It was something I did at first to draw you and hold you. Hypnosis."

"I see," Cole said (though he'd already known, on some level). "But the real reason I asked . . ."

"You want it now?" City said. "You are a sentimentalist."

"No. It just seems right, somehow."

City nodded, and walked across the lawn, spectral and terrible in the glare of the floodlights. A sharply rhythmic, electronic music radiated from him. Cole could *see* the music, from his new perspective. The sound waves criss-crossed one another to form cubistic patterns that comple-mented the musical arrangement nicely.

Cole followed a few paces behind, walking on feathers and clouds.

The dogs leaped onto City the instant he came within reach. Another instant and both of them leaped back howl-ing, blood running from the teeth that had broken on City's unyielding flesh.

The front door opened, and a man with a gun . . . was dead, a split-second after he'd fired the gun, as City pushed his arm through the man's belly as if it were wet cotton.

"Hey, I can't get the back door open!" someone shouted.

"Never mind," someone else shouted as Cole followed

City through the front door and into the cluttered, sweat-stinking living room. Men were running from the room, their backs to Cole, piling half on top of one another down the basement stairs.

"That thing wasted Billy! He's some fucking robot thing!"

"Get the fucking explosives—be careful!"

"Set it to go off and we can go out the basement window—"

"Window's stuck! Can't break it!"

"Hey, don't turn that—"

Cole was halfway down the stairs when the house went up. He rode shock waves and watched flying shards pass harmlessly through him. He wondered if he were passing through them or they through him.

He watched the cascading concrete and wood and plastic and dust and blood with pleasure. The explosion was glorious.

outro

CATZ WAILEN REMOVED THE HEADPHONES. She was alone in the darkened recording studio. The engineer had gone home hours before, trusting Catz to lock up. The only light came from the indicators on the sound board. Her back and sides were soaked in sweat. Her ears rang.

She held her head in her hands and shook with a sudden release of nervous tension. She sobbed, but no tears started from her eyes.

After a while she straightened. In a voice cracked with weariness, she said, "Stu? Are you near me now?"

There was no reply. But something whispered from the darker corners of the room. A vagrant draft, perhaps.

She stood and stretched, making her joints crackle. Then she lay on the rug, full-length, and tried to relax. Her mouth was still, but she called out. She called from someplace deep inside her.

"Thank you, you've bridged to me," Stu said from the skylight window over the studio. She saw his reflection there, but nothing to cast the reflection.

It didn't matter: She could hear him. "Oh Jeezus you

bastard turkey slutter, you sonuvabitch—" She went on like that for a while, and this time tears accompanied the outburst.

The chiaroscuro of Cole in the window smiled faintly till she was done. "Better now?" he asked when she'd lapsed into silence.

"You let him take you," she said flatly. She was sitting up, her legs outstretched on the rug.

"Couldn't help it," Cole said. "But I'm with you. I'm still—"

"Damn! Are you going to give me that I'll-always-be-with-you-in-spirit trash? No credit. I don't *want* you here with me all the time. It'd make me self-conscious. I don't plan to live like a nun grieving over a jelly-spine like you, Cole. I have every intention of getting laid regularly, and I don't want you around invisibly gawking at me."

Cole laughed. Catz didn't.

After a while Cole said, "I had to tell you."

There was bitterness in her tone when she said, "Oh, I understand."

"I've got to go back now."

"I'll bet you do."

"I'm going to help your career. I think I can—"

"Don't do me any favors," she said. She stood and went quickly to the door. On her way out she struck angrily at the sound board, hitting a switch: The recorded music, Catz's band, cascaded like a glorious explosion into the room. Catz was gone. Cole remained for a moment, listening. Then he went to another city, and other music.